SPLURCH ACADEMY

FOR DISRUPTIVE BOYS

THE COLOSSAL FOSSIL FREAKOUT

GROSSET & DUNLAP
Published by the Penguin Group
Penguin Group (USA) Inc., 375 Hudson Street,
New York, New York 10014, USA
Penguin Group (Canada), 90 Eglinton Avenue East, Suite 700,
Toronto, Ontario M4P 2Y3, Canada
(a division of Pearson Penguin Canada Inc.)
Penguin Books Ltd., 80 Strand, London WC2R 0RL, England
Penguin Group Ireland, 25 St. Stephen's Green, Dublin 2, Ireland
(a division of Penguin Books Ltd.)
Penguin Group (Australia), 250 Camberwell Road, Camberwell,
Victoria 3124, Australia
(a division of Pearson Australia Group Pty. Ltd.)
Penguin Books India Pvt. Ltd., 11 Community Centre,
Panchsheel Park, New Delhi—110 017, India
Penguin Group (NZ), 67 Apollo Drive, Rosedale,
North Shore 0632, New Zealand
(a division of Pearson New Zealand Ltd.)
Penguin Books (South Africa) (Pty.) Ltd., 24 Sturdee Avenue,
Rosebank, Johannesburg 2196, South Africa

Penguin Books Ltd., Registered Offices:
80 Strand, London WC2R 0RL, England

Published by Grosset & Dunlap, a division of Penguin Young Readers
Group, 345 Hudson Street, New York, New York 10014.
GROSSET & DUNLAP is a trademark of Penguin Group (USA) Inc.
Printed in the U.S.A.

Typeset in Imprint.

Library of Congress Control Number: 2010034441

ISBN 978-0-448-45361-3 10 9 8 7 6 5 4 3 2

SPLURCH ACADEMY
FOR DISRUPTIVE BOYS

THE COLOSSAL FOSSIL FREAKOUT

by Julie Gardner Berry and Sally Faye Gardner

Grosset & Dunlap
An Imprint of Penguin Group (USA) Inc.

For Delia,
who knows about disruptive boys.
—J.G.B.

For Scott.
—S.F.G.

A Word of Warning to All Disruptive Boys

Are you still here?

Do you really want to know what happens next at Splurch Academy for Disruptive Boys? Weren't you listening when I tried to warn you last time?

Here's a suggestion: Go read a book where kids aren't always narrowly escaping getting eaten.

You're *still* here. I figured you would be.

Clearly you have disruptive tendencies of your own.

Splurch Academy, if you insist, is *supposed* to be a boarding school where boys with challenging behaviors learn in a kind, nurturing environment how to be proper gentlemen. That's what it says in the brochure. It also says the food is delicious.

In truth, Splurch Academy is a scum-lined

cesspool of juvenile misery, where rotten little rascal boys are dropped off and abandoned like yesterday's trash, and never heard from again.

Why, you may ask, if it's so terrible there, don't the boys run away?

Oh, they've tried. Some are still alive to tell the tale.

If you're so smart, how would *you* escape from a school where the headmaster is a vampire? Could you run faster than a teacher who's a werewolf, or a secretary with bat wings and a hawk's beak? How would you break free from the iron grip of a Frankenstein homeroom teacher?

If you've got ideas, I'm sure Cody Mack and his friends would love to hear them.

When last we saw Cody, he'd just accidentally unleashed Dr. Farley from an underground tomb where he'd been sent as a punishment by his ancient mother, the Grand Inquisitrix of the League of Reform Schools for Fiendish Children. The other boys at Splurch Academy were bound to be annoyed with Cody for setting Farley free. But Farley was even more annoyed since Cody had gotten him banished in the first place.

Cody couldn't win.

But by now you know about Splurch Academy. No kid there can ever win.

You'd better pray your parents don't buy you a one-way ticket there.

Grade Five

Possibly the most disruptive bunch of boys Splurch Academy has ever seen.

Cody Mack, age 11

The Master of Disruption. The Sultan of Schemes. The Prince of Plots. The Demigod of Dastardly Deeds. A pint-size Lord of Chaos. The ringleader of the fifth-grade band of brothers, and every teacher's worst nightmare.

Carlos Ferrari, age 10

Cody Mack's best friend. Give him a rubber band, a paper clip, and a can of shaving cream, and he'll turn them into a weapon of mass *disruption*. It's not his fault things tend to blow up when he's around.

Mugsy, aka Percival Porsein, age 11

This kid will eat *anything* as long as it has ketchup on it. Don't tease him about his teddy bear or he'll sit on you. He has a habit of accidentally breaking things, like other people's ribs, but really, he means well.

Ratface, aka Rufus Larsen, age 10

The one kid at Splurch Academy who felt perfectly at home in a rat's body. He's whiny; he's annoying; he has weird ideas. Nothing is safe from this light-fingered little thief.

Sully, aka Sullivan Sanders, age 10

Brave as an earthworm. Athletic as cooked spaghetti. Minus his glasses he's as blind as a mole. Still, being a genius has its advantages. This bookworm won't speak to adults. Period.

Victor Schmitz, age 11

Anger issues got him sent to Splurch, and nothing's changed so far. A good pick for a tug-of-war team, but you don't want to challenge him to an arm-wrestling match. If you do, it's safer if *you* lose.

The Teachers

Dr. Archibald Farley, Headmaster

The egotistical mastermind behind the torture of innocent disruptive boys. With his vampire strength and his mad science cunning, this evil headmaster is never without a plan to make Cody and his friends suffer.

Nurse Bilgewater

Strong as an ox and as kind-hearted as a feeding shark, Beulah Bilgewater is Splurch Academy's medical specialist. Whatever you do, don't get sick. Once this evil nurse gets her tentacles on you, there's no escape.

Mr. Fronk

A lumbering carcass of a fifth-grade teacher who sleeps like a corpse through every class. His two fears: fire and boys who prefer comic books.

Griselda, the Cafeteria Lady

The only thing worse than her cooking is her complaining about her aches and pains. Wait. Never mind. Her cooking's worse.

Mr. Howell

Go ahead. Try to run away from Splurch Academy. This mangy fleabag will even give you a head start. He sprints like a wolf and gnaws on bones for lunch. Better steer clear when the moon comes out . . .

Ivanov, the Hall Monitor

This jack-of-all-trades does the dirty work of keeping the Academy clean. Sort of. He'd rather do the dirty work of tattling on kids.

Librarian

Does she have a name? Does she ever speak? Whose side is she on? No one is sure. But don't raise your voice in her library. Not if you want to own your own tongue.

Miss Threadbare

This bony, spindly, scraggly bag o' knuckles and teeth is Headmaster Farley's secretary by day—a bat-winged hawk-monster by night. Don't be slow when *she* tells you to stand for the pledge.

CHAPTER ONE

THE DIG

Biting November rain slashed Cody Mack's cheeks. It soaked into his prison suit and ran in cold rivers down his back, straight into his underpants.

Just a typical cheerful morning at Splurch Academy.

Cody plunged his shovel into the soggy soil of the trench he'd been digging. Not because he wanted to. The entire monstrous school faculty stood guard to make sure the boys didn't stop digging. Dig or die, those were the choices. Cody heaved a heavy shovelful of mud out of the trench.

OOF!
FWOOSH
SPLOP

WHAT THE . . .
GGRRAAGHH!
OOPS!

Cody huddled as small as he could. *He may eat me,* Cody thought, *but before I die I can whack him a good one with this shovel.*

"Howell. That's enough."

Headmaster Archibald Farley appeared and gave Howell a warning look.

Off in the distance, through the trees, Cody heard the roar of truck engines on the highway. So close . . . the civilized world outside this stinking Academy was so close . . . he could almost taste it. . . . If he could just get to the road, he could hitch a ride on a truck. He'd go anywhere so long as it was far away from here.

Howell wandered off to wipe the mud from his shirt, and Farley strolled away to supervise other boys.

"*Psst.*"

Cody couldn't see who was whispering.

"*Psst.* Cody!"

It was Carlos, digging in his trench.

"Hey, Carlos," Cody said. "You okay?"

"My hands are all blisters," Carlos said. "Yeah. I'm okay."

Sully joined them.

WHAT'S THE DEAL WITH FARLEY'S CLOTHES? IS HE GOING ON A SAFARI?

JUDGING FROM THESE SHOVELS, I'D SAY HE THINKS HE'S AN ARCHAEOLOGIST.
AN ARKY-WHAT-IGIST?

"Someone who digs up stuff from the past," Sully said. "Artifacts. Fossils. Buried treasure."

Carlos laughed softly. "Ha. Like there'd be any buried treasure around *this* dump."

Ratface wiped his dripping nose on his soggy sleeve. "I liked Farley better as a loony scientist," he said.

"I never liked Farley, ever," Victor said.

"Mad science, mad archaeology, it's all the same," Cody said.

"When's he going to let us go eat lunch?" Mugsy moaned. "This dirt's starting to look like chocolate pudding. Why d'you suppose Farley wants us digging all these rectangles, anyway?"

Sully stopped digging. "Isn't it obvious, Mugs?"

Mugsy shook his head. His curly hair wobbled.

Sully shoved his glasses back up his nose. "Don't you guys get it? Look around." Still, Mugsy looked perplexed. So did Cody, for that matter.

"We're digging our own graves."

Nobody even bothered trying to deny it. Farley and the teachers loathed the boys sent to Splurch Academy. The feeling was mutual. There were rules in place that Farley didn't dare openly break—rules that made sure he and the other monsters couldn't kill or eat the boys—but that didn't stop Farley from constantly searching for loopholes around those rules. Ever since he'd returned from his imprisonment in the crypt underneath the Academy where his mother had sent him for bad behavior, he'd been looking for new ways to get around those pesky regulations. Today's digging nonsense probably meant he'd finally found a way.

A sound coming from deep in the woods made Cody and the other boys pause. Through the thinning branches and the pouring rain, someone was running. The person was sprinting over snapping twigs and slick, crunching leaves.

"Who's that?" Cody hissed, pointing. "What's going on?"

"It's Shoffwall," Carlos whispered.

"That big moron from the seventh grade. He's making a break!"

Cody's breath caught in his throat. An escape! Ever since his parents and his principal had sent him to this backwater of misery, Cody had dreamed of nothing else but escape. It wasn't his fault Headmaster Farley and his monster teachers had outfoxed him at every turn. Someday . . .

Run, kid, run, Cody thought. *Bust outta here, and maybe we can be next. Tell your parents. Tell all the parents what an evil school this is!*

Pavlov's bark rang out like a gunshot. All the teachers looked up. They saw Shoffwall. He was almost to the road now.

Oh no. Cody shook his head. *Shoffwall's a goner.*

Farley gestured leisurely to Nurse Bilgewater. "Beulah," he said, "we seem to have a student anxious to get exercise."

Nurse Bilgewater nodded. "I see that."

"Would you be so kind," Farley said, "as to take care of this little problem in your own special way?"

OH, GOODY!

TUMPTY-TUM . . .

BAM!

Shoffwall hit the dirt, inches from the pavement.

Ratface began whimpering. "They killed that kid! They killed that doofus Shoffwall! I've witnessed a murder!"

"Not quite, but almost," Sully said. "That wasn't a normal bullet. It was a turbo electrozap mind-scrambler dart. One of Farley's special inventions."

Mud flew up in the air as the students resumed digging. *Shoonk* went the shovels, slicing through rocky dirt. *Fwish* went the soil, landing in a pile, or in someone else's face. Cody dug like there was no tomorrow, which might have turned out to be the case. Pavlov stalked around their holes, growling at anybody who paused even to wipe the rain off their faces.

Cody climbed down into his trench to dig farther. *Clink* went his shovel. He'd hit something hard. A rock? He jabbed around it with the blade. No, not a rock. It was long and skinny. And pale, too, once he got some of the dirt off.

It was a bone. He bent over and pried it up. Pavlov's growl rumbled in his throat. His murderous eyes smoldered as he glared over the edge of the hole.

Cody looked at the bone, then at Pavlov. "Here, doggy," he cried. "Fetch!" And he flung the bone as far as he could. Pavlov galloped off after it.

Cody watched him go. Pavlov fetched the bone, then trotted over to Farley and dropped it in his master's lap.

Stupid dog, Cody thought. *How could Farley possibly have gotten a dog to like him?*

"Pavlov, old boy, you're mussing up my trousers," Farley said. Then he took a closer look at the bone. He picked it up and polished it on Howell's shirt.

Rising to his feet, he stumbled across the lawn like a man in a daze. He reached Cody's trench and stared right through him as though he weren't there, but then plucked Cody out with one yank of his collar. He might have looked like an old fossil, but he still had superhuman vampire strength.

FRONK, IVANOV, I NEED YOU!

DIG
DIG
DIG
DIG
EUREKA!

AT LAST! I'VE GOT YOU BACK, OLD BOY!

Cody and the other boys stood like bent sticks stuck in the mud, watching the headmaster. *He's a lunatic,* Cody thought. *A complete and total lunatic.*

Cody was cold, wet, and angry. He didn't care what happened to him anymore. Not even if he got locked in the highest tower for a month for sassing the headmaster. It'd be worth it.

"What'd you find in your mud puddle, Farley?" Cody said. "You're acting like you just won the lottery. What's the big fat deal about a stupid little bone?"

"That's *Headmaster* Farley to you, Roadkill Breath," Howell growled.

But Farley only sneered at Cody. He held up a hand to stop Howell from saying more. A slow smile spread over his lips. He held up a jawbone studded with deadly looking teeth. "You'll find out soon enough, Master Mack," he said. "I'll personally make sure you're the first to know."

CHAPTER TWO
THE BONES

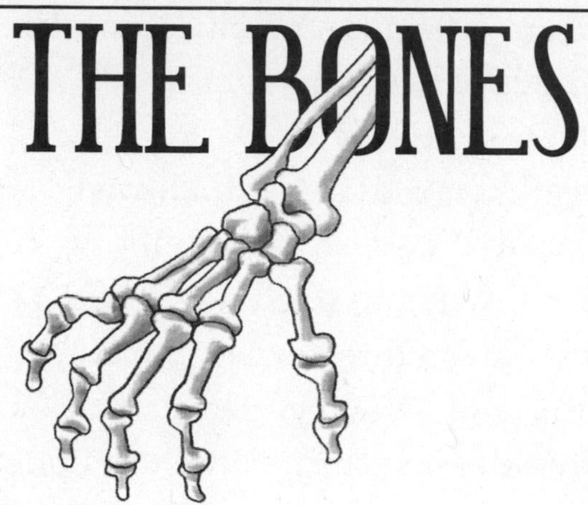

Digging was canceled and the boys were sent back inside the school. They dried off and headed to class.

In the hallway they came across a skeleton propped against the wall.

"What's this?" Sully asked. "Is one of the teachers actually going to teach us some science?"

"Those aren't just any bones," Cody said. "See the tie and the hat? This is Farley's Uncle Rastus, remember?

"Oh yeah," Mugsy said. "We found him in Farley's closet around Halloween."

"What's he doing here?" Cody asked.

Ratface stared at the skeleton. "Is it me or did he just move his hand?"

"Oh, sure, Ratface," Victor said. "Dead bones can just move. On their own. Right."

"Hey, I know a song about bones," Mugsy said. He started singing. "The hip bone's connected to the ear bone . . ."

"It is not, you goofus," Carlos said. "There's no such thing as an ear bone."

"Actually, the inner ear contains three tiny bones, called ossicles, which transmit vibrations from the tympanic membrane."

"Whoa! Cut!" Ratface said. "Too early in the day for your brain waves, Sully. I haven't had my lunch yet."

Victor sniffed the air. "Lunch smells like toxic waste soup."

"Better than the charred skunk burgers we had last week," Ratface replied.

Mugsy rolled his eyes. "They were chicken patties. Not too bad with ketchup."

They went into their classroom. Mr. Fronk sat at his desk, taking a little power nap.

The school bell rang. Fronk's bloodshot eyes opened, and he unclipped his power cords. He looked wearily at the boys and stretched.

"You again?" He rubbed his red eyes. "I was having a beautiful dream. I dreamed that I got to teach students with actual brains. Then I wake up and see you boys here."

"Believe me," Cody said. "We're not any happier about it than you are."

Fronk ignored Cody. He rose to his feet. "If you must be here, then it's time you learned the classics," he told his class.

"They will improve your minds and give you an appreciation for taste and culture."

Cody and his friends stared blankly at Mr. Fronk. Classics, what? Culture, what? A prison sentence at Splurch Academy was bad enough without this sick abuse.

"*Romeo and Juliet* is a good start." Fronk passed out tattered paperbacks.

"A stupid girl book?" Ratface squawked. "He wants us to read a *stupid girl book*?"

"Yeah," Carlos said, laughing. "Only stupid girls would read it!"

"Kissy kissy kissy!" Cody said. "Smoochie-smoo!"

Carlos's laugh froze on his lips when he saw Mr. Fronk glaring at him through yellow eyes.

"You think this is stupid, boys?" He grabbed Sully's copy. "What would maggots like you know? You wouldn't recognize true art if it ate your lunch out from under your nose. The finest minds through the ages have honored Shakespeare for his brilliance. Scholars everywhere can quote him by heart. Listen to this."

BUT, SOFT!
WHAT LIGHT
THROUGH YONDER
WINDOW BREAKS . . .
ROMEO

CRASH
HEY! WHO
DID THAT?!

HEY, MR. FRONK,
"YONDER WINDOW
BREAKS!"
GET IT? GET IT?
YONDER WINDOW
BREAKS?!

Fronk lumbered over to Cody and scowled at him.

"Who did it, Mr. Mack? Tell me now."

Cody shrugged. "Did what?"

"Broke the window!"

"Broke what window?"

Fronk was getting angry now. "*That* window! The one that's broken! Right over there. You just said yourself that . . ."

"Windows all look fine to me," Cody said, crossing his arms over his chest.

Cody could've sworn he saw puffs of steam coming out of Fronk's ears.

Fronk turned to Sully. "Sullivan! You never miss a thing. Tell me who did it!"

Sully didn't even respond. He just stared off into space like he didn't know Fronk was there. He might as well have been a fish. Even though Cody knew Sully never spoke to adults, he was still impressed to see how he pulled it off.

Fronk gave up. "Detention for all you vermin tonight," Fronk said. He left the room, and they heard his booming voice calling for Ivanov to bring his broom.

"'Yonder window breaks . . . .'" Cody high-fived Ratface. "That," he said, "was genius. Sheer genius!"

"I can't believe you were listening that closely," Sully said.

Ratface held his nose high in the air. "The finest minds through the ages know their classics." They all laughed.

"Hey, guys," Cody said, watching the door to make sure Fronk hadn't returned. "After lights-out tonight, let's come back and get Uncle Rastus and bring him to the dorm. He can be our mascot!"

Carlos shrugged. "Why not? It's not like we've got other plans."

Sully shook his head. "If Ivanov catches us out of bed, we're toast."

"We're toast already," Carlos said. "We're stuck at Splurch, remember?"

Mugsy tugged on Cody's sleeve. "But Fronk said we've got detention."

"So, we bust out of detention. What's the big deal? There's no place in this school they can lock us in that our Ratface can't get us out."

"You were saying, Cody?" Sully said. "How's that escape plan coming, Ratface?"

"They can't do this to us!" Ratface said. "It's barbaric! It's primitive! It's gotta be illegal ten times over."

"Like that matters," Cody said.

"Something's dripping on my nose," Victor said.

"It's sewer water," Sully said. "From the pipes."

"This stinks," Mugsy said.

"Oh, come on. Cheer up, guys," Cody said. "We've been worse off than this before. Remember when—"

"No, I mean, the sewer juice stinks," Mugsy said. "Pee-yew."

"Okay, guys, here's the plan," Cody said. "Victor. Mugsy. Use your massive strength

to smash through the wood and set us free."

Victor rattled the stocks. "Yeah, right. Why don't *you* smash through this wood? It's about four inches thick."

"Ratface, haven't you got anything in your pockets to pick a lock with?" Cody asked. "You always do."

"Sure I do," Ratface said. "Can anybody reach my pockets?"

They sat there for a while. Cody's neck chafed against the wooden hole. He couldn't feel his toes. He wished he could go to sleep, but if he didn't hold his head up, he'd choke with his neck resting on the wood.

Then they heard something. Noises. Voices. Sounds of . . . pouring, bubbling liquids? And hissing steam?

"Sully," Carlos whispered. "What's on

the other side of that wall? A kitchen?"

"Farley's laboratory," Sully said. "He must be doing some sort of experiment."

"*Shh,*" Carlos said. "The sounds are coming from that grate. Listen!"

It was Farley's unmistakable voice.

"Yeah," Howell said. "You could sell this baby for a fortune to any museum. We could all take a nice cruise to Transylvania."

"You're babbling!" Farley cried. "Sell him? *Sell* him? I've got much bigger plans for him than to earn mere *money*."

"What plans?"

There was a pause, then a little bang, like a chemistry experiment exploding.

"It's personal." Farley was chuckling now. "And you'll have to wait and see."

CHAPTER THREE

THE AIRPLANE

The scrambled eggs the next morning were less rubbery than usual, and the boys were actually eating their breakfasts when a roaring sound filled the air.

It was an airplane, flying straight toward the Academy building! The boys ran to the windows for a better look.

It was the strangest looking airplane Cody had ever seen. From the puffs of dark smoke and the choking sound the engine made, it seemed like it was going to explode, but still it flew loop-de-loops through the sky, then came in for a landing right across the Splurch Academy lawns. Closer and closer it sped, its wheels tearing up the grass, until the Splurch boys backed away from the window in terror. The plane stopped with its nose just inches away from the window.

Griselda fell down in a dead faint into the garbage can. The boys ignored her. They were watching the pilot and the passengers, dressed in leather helmets and bomber jackets, climb out of the plane.

One passenger climbed out. And then another. And another, and another, and another!

"Where did they all fit?" Sully whispered to Cody.

Five passengers had hopped out from the tiny plane. "It's like the plane is bewitched," Cody answered.

The passengers didn't bother to knock at the Academy entrance.

THE CAFETERIA DOOR OPENED WITH A BANG.
WHAM!

IN CAME THE PILOT AND FIVE KID COMPANIONS.

WHO IS *THAT?*

ZZZIP
JEEPERS! GIRLS!

AND A MONKEY, TOO?

The boys all took a step back. Carlos ran his fingers through his hair. Victor started flexing his muscles, posing to impress the girls! Cody wanted to laugh at them both, but this wasn't the time. First, he needed to find out what was going on.

"Who're you?" he asked the tall woman.

She pulled off her glove, one finger at a time. "That's no way to address your betters," she said. She looked away as if the sight of Cody bored her.

Cody studied the girls. They were about his age, it seemed. *But what were they doing here?* he wondered. Were they the okay kind of girls, or the completely annoying kind?

Generally Cody didn't have much use for girls, but after all, these girls did fly here in a cool plane, and they were wearing neat-o leather jackets. That might be worth something.

One girl met his gaze. He gave her a little half wave.

She scowled at him.

He hadn't done a thing! So much for being friendly . . .

Sully elbowed Cody to warn him to knock it off. The tall woman was frowning down at the boys.

The cafeteria door opened, and the faculty walked in, wearing bathrobes, pajamas, hair curlers, and slippers. The teachers shuffled over to the coffeepot.

Fronk, Nurse Bilgewater, Howell, and Miss Threadbare all looked like they'd seen better days. Only Headmaster Farley was missing.

Then they noticed the newcomers.

Crash! Miss Threadbare's coffee cup shattered on the floor. Nurse Bilgewater choked on a mouthful of sausage.

"What's all this?" Miss Threadbare gasped, pointing a finger at the woman. "Who are you? Who let you in here?"

"Good morning," the woman said, thrusting out a hand. "Priscilla Prim. I've been sent here by the Grand Inquisitrix of the League of Reform Schools for Fiendish Children to organize this school. I brought my pupils with me. We're moving in."

The Splurch teachers looked at one another and busted out laughing.

Priscilla Prim cracked her knuckles. She looked like she was bracing for a battle she planned to enjoy.

WHAT IN
THUNDERATION . . .

. . . DO YOU
THINK YOU
ARE DOING
HERE?

QUITE THE WELCOME YOU OFFER. NO GREETING? NO HUG?

GET YOUR PLANE AND YOUR GRUBBY GIRLS OUT OF MY SCHOOL THIS INSTANT.

HELLO, LITTLE BROTHER.

CHAPTER FOUR

THE GYM

"She's your *sister*?" Howell asked. "You never said anything about a sister."

"My brother, Archibald, doesn't often mention me," Miss Prim said. "I give him an inferiority complex."

Veins bulged in Farley's forehead. "You give me a pain in the neck! Get your little girl scouts out of here. You've got no business here."

The monkey hissed at Farley. Priscilla pulled a folded letter from her inner pocket. "Oh, but I do," she said. "Didn't Mother tell you? She sent me this letter." She read from the parchment. "Darling Priscilla, be a dear girl and go take over Archie's school for a while, won't you? He's been naughty to the boys, so I had to send him to time-out, but sooner or later he'll find a way out. I know I can count on you to tidy up and bring Little Brother's school up-to-date."

Priscilla tucked the letter back into her pocket and smirked at Farley. "Don't worry, Archie-Farchie." She patted him on the head. "I'll fix everything. And I'll take good care of you."

"Whatever you say, Starchy-Archie," Priscilla said. "Come, girls, let's find your rooms."

"Just because you're older doesn't make you the boss of me!" Farley shrieked. "Fronk, take the boys to the gym while I sort this problem out."

"Exercise! An excellent idea," Priscilla cried. "My girls will go to the gymnasium, too. They'll have a jolly time getting acquainted with your boys." She leaned toward her students and whispered. "Go easy on them, girls," she said. "We don't want any of the nice young lads to get hurt."

"We don't want any of the *nice young lads* to get *hurt*," Victor mimicked. "Geez."

They reached the gym. One of the girls picked up a basketball and began to dribble.

The familiar *ping-ping* of a basketball on a hardwood floor was music to Cody's ears. He'd played on a team in his pre-Splurch life. The Galloping Gorillas, they had called themselves. Cody'd been point guard and co-captain. So long ago . . .

MARYBETH, ALLEY-OOP!
WHOOSH!
NICE ONE, ROXANNE!

ALL RIGHT, LADIES. THIS IS OUR GYM. IF ANYONE'S GOING TO PLAY HOOPS, IT'S US.
I DON'T THINK SO. THIS IS OUR HOUSE NOW.

YOU TELL HIM, MARYBETH.
DO YOU GUYS ALWAYS TALK TOGETHER?
WHAT ARE YOUR NAMES, ANYWAY?
BRITTANY AND BROOKE.

"Yeah, but which is which?"

Brittany and Brooke fixed Ratface with an evil sneer. "Wouldn't you like to know?"

Ratface rolled his eyes. "No. I don't want to know either of your stupid names. I just want you to leave. All you crummy girls. Go back to your girls' school and do your . . . ballet and Barbie dolls and whatever. The sooner, the better."

The other boys cheered.

"Yeah," Mugsy cried. "What he said."

But Marybeth and the other tall girl weren't amused.

"This school is filthy. Even the dirt talks. Let's clean up this place, Roxanne," Marybeth yelled, and before Ratface knew what hit him, Marybeth and Roxanne grabbed him by his elbows and stuffed him into a garbage can. Brittany and Brooke grabbed mops and swept Sully's feet out from under him.

"That's it!" Victor yelled. "Nobody sticks my friends in the trash. This means war. To the death!"

A bossy-looking girl stepped forward.

I'M VIRGINIA. LET'S PLAY TO SEVEN. DON'T WORRY, WE'LL GO EASY ON YOU.
HA. GAME ON!
SULLY THREW UP THE JUMP BALL.
WHOOSH!
TWO POINTS, PRISCILLA PRIM.

Cody brought the ball up the court and began directing his team where to go. "We've got to set up a play, men," he said, pointing Victor and Mugsy toward the center and getting ready to pass to Carlos. "Move around. Stay open. You—"

Whoosh.

One of the twins snagged the ball right out from under his dribble and passed it to Roxanne. She sprinted toward the unguarded basket. A perfect breakaway.

"Time-out!" Cody yelled. He and the other boys huddled with Sully.

"I've drawn up some plays," Sully began, producing a clipboard from who knows where, covered with *X*'s and *O*'s.

"Never mind that," Cody said. "Guys, come on! Are you gonna just stand by and let those Priscilla Poo-heads make you look like idiots?"

"If we ever got our hands on the ball, we would," Ratface said. "I mean, you can't even seem to hold onto it without one of them picking it out from under your nose like a booger."

Suddenly, Miss Threadbare's voice came screeching over the loudspeaker. "MR. FRONK AND STUDENTS, REPORT TO CLASSES."

Mr. Fronk, who had been sleeping through the entire ball game, began to stir in his chair.

"Looks like we won," Virginia said. "We've got four points, and you've got . . . what? A big goose egg?" She clicked her tongue. "What a shame."

Victor scowled at her. "You didn't *win*. We barely even got started. We were about to chop you into dog food." Victor grabbed a ball and made a sweet shot.

"MR. FRONK WILL BE TEACHING THE GIRLS IN HIS CLASS THIS AFTERNOON," Miss Threadbare's voice added.

Fronk scowled. He headed for the door. "C'mon, toads. Let's go."

Cody gestured toward the other guys to follow him to class and leave the girls behind.

"So," Cody whispered. "Looks like Farley hasn't thought up a way to get rid of his sister."

"Yet," Sully added.

"Lamebrain Farley can't think his way out of a paper bag," Victor said.

"Then I say," Cody added, "we'll have to get rid of the girls ourselves."

CHAPTER FIVE

THE CHALLENGE

Having the girls around made detention feel like an all-night spree in a candy factory. With the girls in his fifth-grade classroom, Mr. Fronk decided to stage a live performance of the balcony scene from *Romeo and Juliet*.

"Here are your lines," Fronk said, passing them each sheets of paper. "Put some feeling into them! Here, young lady. You need to be on a balcony. Stand here on this chair. And, Mr. Mack, you'll be here, hiding in the bushes and watching Juliet. But she doesn't know you're there."

OH, ROMEO, ROMEO. WHEREFORE ART THOU, ROMEO?
I THINK I'M GONNA BARF!

"Nice tights, Cody," Victor hooted.

"Watch it, buster," Cody snarled.

"Stick to the script," Fronk demanded, "or we'll make this a silent play and go straight for the passionate kissing."

Fortunately for Cody, the bell rang, saving him from having to choose between kissing a girl or facing the wrath of an undead corpse teacher.

When they got to lunch, not only had the girls commandeered the boys' usual table, but Griselda had made all the girls fresh fruit salads, milk shakes, and chicken sandwich wraps. She'd even put a flower in a vase on their table. For the boys, it was the usual Splurchy fare—possum sloppy Joes on pumpernickel buns. And they had to sit on the floor to eat it.

"I thought this place could get no worse," Mugsy moaned. He covered his sloppy possum with ketchup and took a forlorn bite. "How come we don't get milk shakes?"

"Because Griselda's playing favorites with the girls, just like Priscilla Prim does," Sully said.

"If Farley was looking to make our lives more miserable, he couldn't have done better than bringing those girls here," Carlos said. "Are you sure he wasn't behind it somehow?"

"Nah," Cody said. "Farley hates his sister like a cat hates a bath."

In the hallways, the boys saw two of the girls prowling around with magnifying glasses, studying every brick, every tile, and every board in the old Academy.

After classes and dinner, the boys returned to their dorm.

"At least there's one place in this rotten school where we can still get away from the girls," Victor said. "Our dorm room."

"Yeah," Ratface said. "Our sanctuary, where females dare not go. The one place we can safely plot and plan how to get rid of them forever."

But when they reached their room, they found a sign on the door marked "Private. Keep Out!"

"Huh?" Ratface said.

They opened the door and a pillow came flying at them.

"Go away, foul intruders!" a girl's voice shrieked.

The door slammed in Cody's face.

Cody's jaw dropped. He pounded on the door with his fists.

The door opened.

"You can't come in," Brittany and Brooke told the boys. "This is our room now. It's extremely private."

"No it isn't, it . . ." Cody never finished his sentence. The sight that met his eyes made him want to puke. There, in their old bedroom, were more shades of pink than on a lipstick display counter and more flowers than on a coffin.

The girls had decorated the dorm.

"All the other rooms were unsuitable," Marybeth told Cody and the boys. "Miss Prim said we were welcome to take this one. She told us we were free to decorate any way we liked."

"There was a bunch of crummy junk in the bunks," Virginia added. "It smelled bad. We threw it all away."

"You *what*?" Ratface shrieked. "All my stuff? Gone?"

"It was rubbish," Virginia said with a shrug. "We did you a favor by getting rid of it."

"You'll pay for this," Victor said, shaking his fist. "You can't just kick us out!"

"Watch us." Brittany and Brooke pushed the boys out and slammed the door.

Ivanov, the hunchbacked hall monitor, hobbled down the hall and led the boys to their new sleeping quarters—a cold, drafty room that used to be the stables, once upon a time when the Splurch Academy grown-ups had horses pulling their carriages and wagons. The floor of each stall was covered with a layer of moldy, stinky straw. A few lucky boys found rope hammocks to sleep in.

"We need to hold a council of war," Carlos said grimly.

"Sure, but it's almost dark," Cody said, looking out the window. "Griselda's probably gone to bed. Want to go raid the kitchen?"

They tiptoed through the shadowy hallways. At the sound of clicking heels on the stone floor, they froze and drew back against the wall.

It was Priscilla Prim, with a duster in her hand. She opened a closet door and began nosing through, remarking in disgust at the clutter inside.

"What's this?" she cried. "Who's hiding in there?"

She stepped back into the hallway, holding a skeleton by the arms.

Priscilla propped him against the wall and dusted him off. Then she paused and took a closer look at his necktie and hat.

"Why, bless my bunions," she said. "It's Uncle Rastus! You poor old thing. Why are you stuffed in a closet? You should be down in the nice, quiet crypt with Aunt Rhoda! I'll just take you there right now."

She tucked him under one arm, turned, and let out a little shriek.

"Not so fast, my meddlesome sister." It was Farley, silhouetted in the dim light at the end of the hall, glowering at Priscilla. "Drop the bones."

"You can jolly well bet I won't," Priscilla retorted. "Uncle Rastus isn't yours. He's his own skeleton. He deserves a peaceful rest down in the crypt with his wife."

Farley seized Uncle Rastus's arm. "I keep him around for . . . sentimental reasons. I'll just take him now."

Priscilla pulled back on Rastus's other arm. "Sentimental hogwash! You haven't got a tender bone in your body. Have you no respect for your own uncle's remains?"

Farley smirked. "I have the utmost respect for his remains. That's why I need to keep him around." Uncle Rastus's ribcage rattled from the tug-of-war between Farley and Priscilla. "Good of you to locate him for me just now. He'd wandered off again."

"Nonsense!"

Farley wrenched Uncle Rastus out of Priscilla's grasp. "Got him!" The skeleton collapsed into a heap of bones. Farley scooped him up in his arms. "Oh, and sister dear? Since you're so eager to be in charge of the student brats, I turn the reins of the school over to you. I'll be busy in my laboratory working on my research."

Priscilla snatched at the piles of bones, but Farley held them out of her reach. "You've always managed this school by neglecting it," she said.

"La-la-la-la," Farley retorted. "I'm not listening."

"You'll be listening when Mother shows up," Priscilla shot back. "I've mailed her a letter listing the atrocities I see. Poor nutrition, nonexistent education, appalling hygiene, no arts, no culture, no athletic opportunities for these poor boys. . . . Why, they're spineless wimps! My girls could mop the floors with your measly, puny, malnourished boys!"

"Who's she calling puny?" Mugsy whispered.

"Yeah," Victor growled. "Spineless wimps? I'll show her . . ."

At the mention of his mother, Farley's eyebrows twitched. Then he smiled.

"I'll take that as a challenge," he said. "A match between our students to show Mother which school is truly supreme."

"I accept your challenge. With pleasure," Priscilla said. "Which sport shall it be?"

"Kickboxing," Farley said.

"Awesome!" Victor whispered.

"You're out of your mind," Priscilla said.

"Mud wrestling," Farley said.

"No, you imbecile," Priscilla said. "Something civilized. That's why athletics were invented. How about field hockey?"

"Fine," Farley said. "But if we're doing sports, we're doing them old Splurch style." He opened the door to his laboratory.

Priscilla nodded. "All's fair in love and war?"

"War, anyway," Farley said.

"Whoever loses will tell Mother how wonderful the other one is." Priscilla rubbed her hands together.

"Fair enough," Farley said. "But also, whoever loses will *leave*."

They stomped off in different directions. The boys stared at one other.

"Um, Cody?" Ratface whispered. "So whose side are we on? Farley's or Miss Prim's?"

"Neither," Cody declared. "We're only on our side. All for one and one for all!"

"Right—like that candy bar," Mugsy said. "The, uh, Three Amigos?"

"The Three Musketeers." Sully rolled his eyes. "So do we try to win the game and get rid of the girls, or do we lose the game and get rid of Farley?"

"Tough choice," Cody said. "I say we escape before the game ever happens."

Victor folded his arms across his chest. "Right. Like that'll work."

"Sure it will," Cody said.

"Well, in case we don't escape," Victor said, "I say we clobber them. No way am I going to let those slimy girls beat us at sports. Besides, girls just plain don't belong at Splurch Academy. Period."

CHAPTER SIX

THE MONKEY

The next morning the girls confronted Cody and his friends after breakfast.

"We heard about the field hockey game," Marybeth said. "Get ready to lose, boys. You haven't got a prayer."

"Guess again, cream puffs," Victor growled. "The other day? That basketball game? We weren't even trying. We didn't want to hurt your feelings."

"Ha," Roxanne said. "That's a good one. We annihilated you. And by the way, the Priscilla Prim field hockey team came in second in States this year."

"Hygiene inspection!"

It was Miss Prim coming around the corner wearing a special set of glasses with telescoping lenses.

"Hold out your fingernails, please!"

The boys held out their hands. The girls stayed to watch. Miss Prim grasped Mugsy's wrist to examine his hand closely.

"Never," she said, "in my decades of teaching, have I ever, *ever* encountered such filth. You. Show me your ears."

She seized Victor's ear and stuck a lighted probe inside it.

"There's so much wax in here, you must have difficulty hearing," she said.

"Hellooooo! Can you hear me, young man?"

Victor rubbed his ears. "Ow!"

"How come you don't hygiene-check the girls?" Cody protested. In reply, Miss Prim began leafing through strands of his hair using two Popsicle sticks.

"Lice check," she snapped. "The good news is your hair is so greasy, the lice just slip right out. I can't say the same for the cockroaches."

Cody scratched his scalp.

"All you boys, report to the infirmary after morning classes for a pressure washing. Chop-chop, girls. Off to class." She strode down the hall, searching for more Splurch boys to torment.

Brittany and Brooke stuck out their tongues at the boys. They left, still testing every brick to see if it was loose, every wooden panel to see if it was a trick one.

"What are they searching for, anyway?" Carlos asked.

"Probably fairies," Ratface sneered.

"Let's find out," Cody said. He took off running after them.

HEY, VIRGINIA, WHAT ARE YOU GUYS LOOKING FOR, ANYWAY?
NOTHING THAT CONCERNS YOU.

IF WE KNEW WHAT YOU WERE LOOKING FOR, MAYBE WE COULD HELP.
WHY DO YOU WANT TO HELP ALL OF A SUDDEN?

WHAT'S THE CATCH?
FORGET IT. IT'S JUST THAT WE'VE FOUND SOME HIDDEN . . . OH, NEVERMIND.

He turned and walked away, but gave his friends a wink.

Sure enough, Virginia grabbed him by the arm.

"You've found hidden . . . what?"

Cody shrugged. "Oh, nothing. Come on, guys. Let's go."

Virginia hesitated, then spoke.

"The problem is," she said, "we don't know exactly what we're looking for ourselves. But we know it's hidden in a top secret place. And we're pretty sure we'll recognize it when we see it."

Wheels were spinning in Cody's head. Here was a great chancc to mess with their heads. "So, you're looking for, like, hidden compartments and stuff?"

Carlos caught Sully's eye and grinned. Cody could tell his friend knew what he was thinking.

Cody patted Virginia on the back. This was going to be fun. "Now, the thing you need to understand about Splurch Academy is, it's haunted."

Mugsy's jaw dropped. Ratface's eyes

bugged out. Cody worked hard not to laugh. Even his friends believed him!

"It's under dozens of ancient magical spells," he continued. "So, the trapdoors and hidden stuff aren't always there. They're only there sometimes. So don't give up if you go to a spot and you don't find any evidence of trapdoors and stuff. You just have to keep trying."

Virginia frowned. "How do we know you're not totally tricking us?"

"You don't know," Cody said. "You'll just have to take our word for it."

"And why should we trust a bunch of dirty, stinking, disruptive boys?" Roxanne demanded.

Ratface pulled a straw and some bits of paper from his pocket. "Watch this," he whispered to Carlos. "Those snooty girls deserve the spit wad treatment." He filled his cheeks with wads of spitty paper.

"You should trust us because . . . ," Cody began, but then the girls started shrieking.

Thut! Thut! Thut! Ratface peppered the girls with machine gun–style spit wads.

THUT
THUT
THUT

YEEEEAAAAAAH!
STOP IT, YOU LITTLE CREEP!
...ATTACK!

HELP! CALL OFF YOUR PET MONKEY!
SCREEECH!
SHE'S NOT JUST OUR PET. SHE'S OUR BODYGUARD.

Virginia wiped the spit wads off her face. "She always knows if someone's trying to hurt one of us," she said. "So don't mess with any of us."

"Yeah," Brittany and Brooke added. "Not if you want to live."

"Oooh," Cody sneered. "I'm so scared. What is she, about twelve pounds?"

"That's enough, Princess," Virginia said. "Let the rat boy go."

"Princess?" Carlos said. "A girl monkey?"

"Why not?" Marybeth said. "Get this straight, Splurchies: Girls rule, boys drool."

Mugsy retorted, "Oh yeah? Well . . . boys are awesome and girls . . . are possums!"

"Nice," Marybeth said. "Wow. You're so smart, I just have no response to that one."

And, laughing, the girls turned and left.

"Ha! 'Girls rule, boys drool,'" Ratface mimicked. "They rule the kingdom of Loser-ness, maybe."

Victor folded his arms over his chest. "We'll show them who rules," he said. "And when we do, it won't be pretty."

"They'll go flying out of here in their stupid plane so fast," Ratface added, "they'll make a sonic zoom."

"Sonic boom," Sully corrected him.

"Yeah, that's what I said," Ratface said.

"All the same," Mugsy replied. "Memo to me: Stay away from the monkey."

CHAPTER SEVEN

THE BATHROOM

"FIRE!"

Cody covered his face with his arms.

Four hundred gallons of water blasted from Miss Threadbare's fireman's hose and hit him full force, nearly knocking him over. It plastered his uniform to his body. His skin felt like it was peeling off.

Then it stopped.

"Bombs away, Tessie!"

Miss Threadbare pulled a chain, and Cody looked up just in time to see an avalanche of frothy soap suds fall from buckets near the ceiling onto their heads.

Nurse Bilgewater, wearing Wellington boots and a snorkel mask, walked up the line, lathering and scrubbing the boys' heads with a long-handled brush.

Another blast of water washed away the suds, followed by a wind tunnel of cold air, which dried the boys off. Sort of. It made all their hair stand up straight. They were still shivering as they left the infirmary.

It had been a gruesome afternoon. Co-ed dance lessons had begun, and each Splurch boy had to tango with a Priscilla Prim girl. When the boys refused to dance with the girls, Priscilla Prim forced them to dance with *her*. She smelled like ancient lilac perfume. And breath mints. Breath mints that couldn't hide the bad breath underneath.

And now this cold pressure wash. Like walking through a car wash. Those rotten girls and their rotten headmistress!

Speaking of girls, there was the small matter of revenge to attend to.

"People are still at dinner, and Farley's in his lab, right?" Cody said.

"Should be," Sully said. "Why?"

Cody grinned. "Let's go."

They broke into Farley's private room and raided his bathroom. In the medicine cabinet they found just what they were looking for.

"Geezer Cream?" Carlos said. "What on earth does he do with Geezer Cream?"

"You don't wanna know," Ratface said.

"Laxo Cleanse?" Cody said. "Nose Drops? I don't ever, *ever* want to get old."

"The longer we stay at Splurch, the less likely we are to live that long," Sully said.

"And *that's* supposed to be comforting?" Ratface snorted. "Thanks a lot."

"What are we doing with all this stuff, anyway, Cody?" Mugsy said.

Cody grinned. "We're going to get back at those girls for stealing our dorm room so bad, they won't ever mess with us again."

Mugsy scratched his head. "With Nose Drops?"

Cody smiled an evil grin. "With all the squirty, slimy, gooey, grody stuff we can find. With toilet paper. With mop water. With shaving cream. Nothing will be safe. Their pillows. Their sheets. Their shoes. They'll never see it coming. Then, whammo!"

"Awesome!" Ratface said. "I've taught you well, young Cody."

"Young Cody nothing," Cody said. "I was a pro before I ever met you."

They sprinted to their old dorm.

"Ugh, these sheets smell like fabric softener," Ratface said. "Pew."

"My mom used to use fabric softener," Mugsy added, and his lower lip began to tremble.

"Steady, Mugsy," Cody warned.

"Too bad we can't stay and watch them find all this stuff," Ratface said.

"Do you really think we can make them leave before the game?" Carlos asked. "That Priscilla Prim is pretty tough. She won't give up easily."

"Don't you remember what happened when we tried to steal Farley's Cadillac?" Ratface asked. "Smash-ola! We nearly got killed. You think stealing a plane is going to work better? You don't know how to fly!"

"We weren't nearly killed," Cody said. "We almost got away! Without even knowing how to drive. We were close. If we'd had a plane, we'd have made it for sure. This time maybe Sully could find us a book on flying from the library. We can become experts before we ever climb into the driver's seat."

"Cockpit," Sully corrected. "Cody, you can't learn to fly from a book. It takes hundreds of hours of practice to get your pilot's license."

"Who needs a *license*?" Cody said. "I'm not worried about getting a stupid ticket. This is a one-way trip. I just want to get home."

Mugsy sighed. "*Home*. It's like I'd forgotten the word."

"Yeah," Carlos said. "Me too."

“Imagine us just flying home,” Ratface said as if he were half asleep. “Just flying through the air, landing in our own backyards, and saying, ‘Mom, Dad! Sorry about the lawn, but it’s great to see you!’ ”

“They’d get mad at me,” Victor said. He scowled. “They’d say, ‘How come you’re not at that reform school? We paid good money for you to be there.’ ”

“They wouldn’t say that if you explained everything to them.” Carlos patted Victor’s back. “Then they’d understand.”

“Or they’d say I was making it up,” Victor said.

"I would rather deal with persuading my parents than deal with staying alive at Splurch Academy," Cody said. "Once we're out of here, our biggest problems are behind us."

Sully looked at the clock. "Those girls'll be back here any minute," he warned.

"C'mon, guys, we'd better get out of here before they come back," Cody said. "Let's scoot."

CHAPTER EIGHT

THE TOENAILS

Cody woke up the next morning in his moldy manure straw bed to see a sign draped across the stables:

THIS MEANS WAR.

The girls had drawn pictures of each of the boys with *X*'s through them.

"Guys, look at this," Cody cried. "The girls left us a thank-you note."

He climbed out of his stall and kicked at where Carlos lay sleeping in the straw. "Wake up, 'Los!"

Then the sight of his own foot made him freeze in terror.

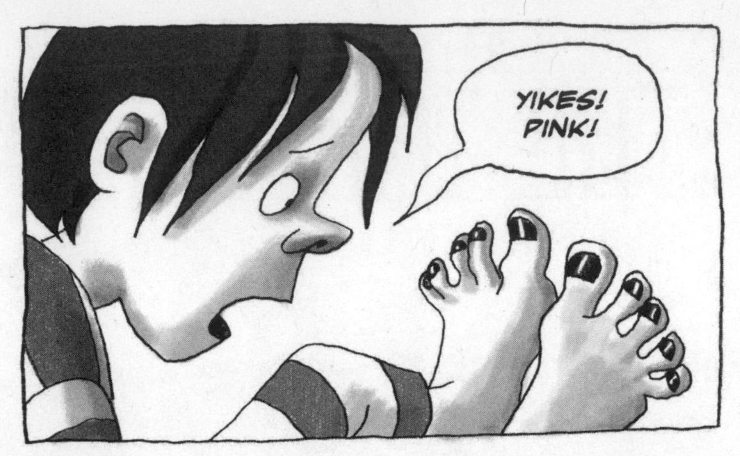

"What's up, Cody?" Carlos murmured, rubbing the sleep from his eyes. Cody buried his toes in the straw. Then he noticed Carlos's toes. They were the same.

"I had the weirdest dream," Mugsy said. "I dreamed I went with my mom to the beauty parlor, and she . . . *aaaauugggh*!"

Everyone had hot-pink nails.

"They did this to us," Cody fumed. "Those Priscilla Prim freaks! They're gonna pay for this."

Sully tried chipping at his toenails with a sliver of rock, but all he did was hurt himself. "I suppose they thought they were paying *us* back for what we did to their room."

"*Our* room," Cody said. "Never forget it's *our* room. They swiped it from us. They started this whole thing. *They're* the bad guys. We're the good guys."

"Technically, they're the bad *girls*," Sully said.

"Both," Ratface said. "Pushy females, always barging in where they're not invited! Farley never invited his sister. How do you get this stuff off?"

"We're not on Farley's side all of a sudden, are we?" Victor said. "It takes some special chemical to get it off."

"We're on nobody's side but ours," Cody declared.

"We can hide our feet inside our—hey! They stole our *shoes*!" Ratface shrieked.

"And our socks," Mugsy said.

"New uniforms?" Ratface asked. "What's wrong with these?"

The boys trudged to Miss Threadbare's office. Miss Prim and the girls waited by a table piled high with new uniforms.

Cody looked down at his toes. He could show Miss Prim exactly what Virginia had done, but he decided he'd rather not.

"Sorry," Cody mumbled.

The headmistress nodded. "That will do. Girls, please issue the boys their new clothes and shoes. In order to get your new shoes, please give us your old ones."

Cody and the boys looked at one another.

"Um, Miss Prim, ma'am," Carlos said. "We don't have any shoes."

"Why not?" The headmistress frowned. "The other boys had shoes."

"Ours were stolen," Carlos said, glaring at Marybeth.

Priscilla peered at the boys. "A likely story. I cannot reward irresponsibility like this. You'll get no new shoes until you produce your old ones. If this means you go barefoot, let that be a lesson to you. I have no time to trifle with inter-student rivalries. Go inside and change clothes."

They went into the changing rooms next to Miss Threadbare's office and squirmed into their new uniforms.

They met up in the hallway.

"Not a stripe in sight!" Ratface said. "We look like total dweebs."

"The old uniforms were way more comfortable," Victor added.

Priscilla Prim poked her head in. "Tie your ties properly . . . there."

Cody hadn't worn a collared shirt and tie since his great-uncle's funeral, long before coming to Splurch Academy. It made him feel choked, like he could barely breathe.

Miss Prim clapped her hands. "Listen up, everybody, today we clean the school from top to bottom. Seventh-graders will climb up to the chandeliers in the faculty lounge and polish the brass and crystal," she said. "Sixth-graders will dust the bookshelves in the library. Fifth-grade girls will sweep the corridors and fifth-grade boys will mop them on hands and knees."

"Like *that's* fair," Victor muttered. "They sweep, we scrub."

Miss Prim didn't hear him. "Ivanov will distribute your brooms, buckets, and sponges here."

"Faculty, this way," Priscilla Prim said. "You will paint my bedroom, varnish all my furniture, and fix the plumbing in my bathroom. Come along! Busy hands make happy hearts!"

The faculty looked ready to rip Miss Prim limb from limb. The girls began sweeping the front entranceway, while the boys tested their sponges to see how much sudsy water they'd hold. Quite a lot, as it turned out.

"You guys got the same idea I've got?" Cody whispered.

"Aw, Cody, don't. We'll only get in huge trouble," Sully whimpered.

READY?
AIM?

FIRE!

SPLAT
SPLAT
SPLAT
SPLAT
SPLAT

"Listen to 'em scream!" Cody laughed.

"They look like wet rats." Ratface snorted with laughter.

"That'll teach you to paint our toes," Victor said.

The wet sponges came sailing back. They were followed by six furious girls wielding brooms like ninja poles.

Cody held up his bucket. "Bring it on, ladies," he said, taunting them with his suds. "We ain't afraid of you."

"That's because you're stupid," Virginia hissed. "One, two, three, ATTACK!"

Whoosh! Arcs of hot, steaming bubbles intersected with whirling broomsticks. *Whap! Whap!* Broomsticks connected with arms and legs and bare pink toes. Girls skidded on suds, boys skated on sponges. When Priscilla Prim arrived, every single fifth-grader was soaking wet, bruised, and filthy.

"They started it, Miss Prim," Marybeth hollered.

"Liar!" Ratface shrieked. "You stole our school!"

The monkey pounded her chest and screamed a primal scream at Cody.

"There, there, sweetie." Priscilla patted her pet monkey. "Good, Princess. The girls are all right." She gave Princess a breath mint, then ate one herself.

Then she scowled at the boys. "I can see that years of my brother's neglect hasn't done you wretched boys any favors. A day's detention in the stocks should do the trick, while I plan a proper punishment."

"You're just like your brother," Cody said.

Miss Prim sucked in her breath. *That*

got her. She shook it off.

"Girls, run along and fetch yourselves a change of clothes. Bandage up your wounds, then take a rest until you feel like resuming the day's activities."

"No way!" Cody yelled. "You can't play favorites like that!"

"Oh, can't I?" Miss Prim tapped her long fingernail on Cody's chin. "*I* can do whatever I want. To the stocks."

"I'm afraid that won't be possible now, sister dear," said a voice. Priscilla Prim turned slowly.

There stood Farley. Howell was beside him, wearing gym shorts and a whistle around his neck. "It's time to begin the boys' field hockey training. I'm afraid they haven't got time for detention today."

"But they require a punishment," Priscilla fumed. "They have it coming!"

"Oh, rest assured, dear sister," Farley said. "Coach Howell will make sure they get exactly what is coming to them."

CHAPTER NINE

THE RUNAWAY

"Take a ten-mile run," Howell barked. "Anyone who lags behind answers to me."

"You didn't just say ten miles, did you?" Mugsy asked. "Maybe, like, ten meters?"

"Yo. Mr. Howell. Dog man," Ratface said. "It's hockey. Not track. Let's not bother with all this running. Shouldn't we, like, hit the puck with the racket or something?"

"What'd you call me?" Howell growled.

Ratface took a step back. "Dog man?" he said. "It's a compliment. Right? For you."

"Zip it, mutt," Howell said. "Okay. Mark. Set. Go."

Running ten miles meant looping around the Academy grounds over and over and over and over and over and over again. Over the lawns, through the woods, past the stream, and into the murky swamp. Coach Howell jogged along easily. Sometimes he got distracted by squirrels and bounded off, and sometimes he stopped to scratch behind his ears, but he always came back and caught up with the boys.

Cody's entire body was one huge cramp. His lungs burned, his legs ached, and his bare feet were pink with nail polish and red with blood from the tiny cuts he got on grasses and twigs.

Once Victor tripped over a stick hidden in the grass. He rose to his feet, muttering,

and flung the stick far away.

Mr. Howell, who was chewing out Sully for being lazy, paused. His eyes followed the stick. His tongue lolled from his mouth. And before he could say "Pick up the pace, lazybones," he was off like a shot, tearing up the grass, chasing after the stick.

The boys gasped at one another.

"Did you just see what I saw?" Sully said.

Howell came trotting back with the stick in his mouth, looking very proud of himself. At the sight of the boys staring at him, his face grew red. He spat out the stick and tried to pretend nothing had happened. He and the boys shuffled off, jogging.

Cody's mind was spinning. Would it work again?

SPLAT

Ratface and the other boys doubled over laughing.

"Guys?" Sully said. "You might want to run. Now."

"I'm sick of running," Mugsy protested. But Sully took off sprinting faster than Cody would have thought possible. He turned and saw a muddy Howell come racing after them.

"It's gonna be a long practice," Carlos panted, falling into step beside Cody.

It was all the boys could do to crawl back into the Academy when practice was over.

After dinner, Cody limped down the hall and passed by the cafeteria. Griselda came out carrying a covered dinner tray.

"Oh. You. Boy. Take this to Farley."

Cody was too tired to protest or think up an excuse. He made his way down the hall and knocked on Farley's laboratory door with his foot. His wobbly arms could barely balance the tray straight.

There was no answer. But Cody could tell Farley was inside. He could hear him grumbling at something.

He kicked the door again. “Coming!” came a yell from within.

Farley wrenched the door open and poked his head out. “What? Who? Oh.” He looked down and noticed Cody. “What do you want?”

“Nothing,” Cody said. “Griselda sent me with your dinner.”

Farley slipped out and pulled the door shut tight behind him. His clothes were ripped and tattered, his skin scratched. He looked like he’d lost a bad fight with a food processor.

Farley ignored him and lifted the lid off the tray. "Ah. Soup." He took a few slurpy bites of soup while Cody still held the tray on trembling arms. "That'll do. Take this back to the kitchen. A man of science has little time for simple pleasures like eating."

"I didn't think you ate people food, anyway," Cody said, stalling. "You know. Right? I mean, I thought you ate people *as* food. Generally speaking."

Farley took one more bite of soup. "How I long for the day when I never need to listen to the obnoxious prattle of another delinquent boy."

The door behind Farley opened silently. Something reached out. Farley wasn't aware of it. Cody tried to think of some way to delay Farley so he could get a better look at it.

It was a hand. A hand of bleached bones.

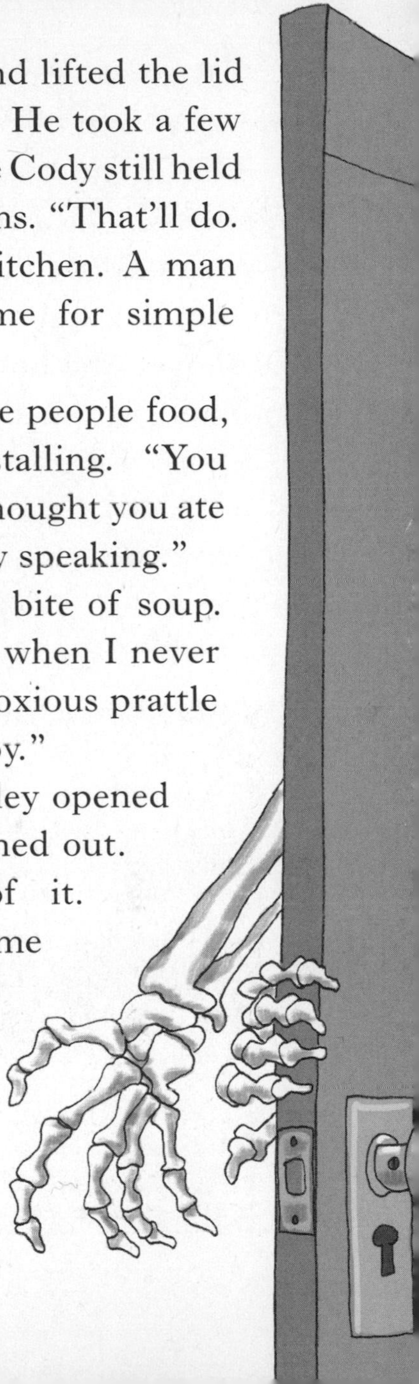

"Well, we all have our dreams," Cody said. "We don't like listening to you, either."

That hand . . . that elbow . . . that shoulder . . . it had to be Uncle Rastus!

Farley noticed Cody staring and whipped around. An annoyed look crossed his face. He shoved the bony arm back through the door and slammed it shut.

CHAPTER TEN

THE CAGE

"Those crummy girls," Mugsy moaned. "We really need to get our shoes back. Everywhere I walk in this disgusting school, bugs go *crunch* under my feet."

"Yeah," Ratface said, "and rat poop goes *squish*."

Cody lay in his pile of stinky straw and stared up into the darkness. His body was sore and his mind was weary. Uniforms, girls, hockey games, skeletons . . . it was too much to sort out. What he'd give, right now, to be back home! To take a hot bath in his own bathroom and wash off all this

Splurchy grossness, then crawl into his own bed and go to sleep. His dog, Snarfy, would curl up at the foot of his bed. Poor Snarfy! He must have been so lonely with Cody gone. Sure, his parents had sent Cody here, telling themselves that this impressive academy for troubled boys would do wonders for *their* disruptive son. But Snarfy? He wouldn't understand any of that. He'd just feel abandoned.

Like Cody.

The other boys were just as miserable. They brooded on revenge.

"Do you realize what a nightmare it would be if she actually ran this place?" Carlos said. "She doesn't want to improve anything. She only wants to spoil her girls, torture us boys, and make Farley mad."

"She wants to turn us *into* girls," Ratface said. "She's a monster!"

Sully sighed. "What else is new? All the teachers at Splurch Academy are monsters. It's in the rules."

Cody kept thinking of the bony hand reaching through Farley's door.

"Hey, guys," he said, sitting up in the straw, "let's go check out what Farley's working on in his lab. Whatever it is, I don't think it's good news for us."

"What if he catches us?" Sully asked.

"It's dark," Cody said. "He'll be out hunting. Ratface, can you still pick a lock?"

"Does Griselda cook with rotten meat?" Ratface retorted. "Of course I can."

They tiptoed through the halls to Farley's lab. Cody listened at the door.

"Nobody's in there," he whispered.

Ratface picked the lock. They went in.

"I can't see what would have chewed Farley to pieces in here." Carlos fingered the science equipment. "Look at all this stuff! What do you suppose he's making?"

"A bomb, I'll bet," Ratface said.

"Not a bomb," Mugsy said. "Just some new way to make our lives miserable."

Carlos was fascinated by Farley's lab. "Geez, I'd love to mess around with *this* chemistry set. I wonder what this button does?"

"Don't just go pressing random buttons!" Sully said.

But Carlos pressed the button, anyway. The floor rumbled. A crack appeared, then an opening.

"That's it. You pressed the self-destruct button," Sully said, backing away as far as he could.

Slowly, slowly, a table on a pedestal rose from beneath the floor. The table was cluttered with wires, papers, meters, a strange device, and something large covered with a cloth drape. And bones. A heap of animal bones.

WHAT IN THE NAME OF KETCHUP IS THAT?
I'D SAY IT LOOKS LIKE A SMALL, CARNIVOROUS DINOSAUR. A FAST ONE. A FEROCIOUS ONE.

MONGRELOSAURUS SPLURCHIUS

"Mon-grel-o-what?" Mugsy sounded out the words.

"I've never heard of that dinosaur before," Sully said.

Carlos was more interested in the device. "Animatrometer," he read. "I wonder what it measures." He followed the electrical cables. "Where do these go . . . oh!"

He yanked off the drape. Underneath was a tall, glass dome.

Inside the dome was Uncle Rastus. If ever a skeleton looked down in the dumps, this one did.

Cody tried lifting the dome, but it seemed sealed shut. He tapped on the glass. "Hey, Uncle Rastus," he called. "What's the matter? C'mon, you can tell us."

"Oh, sure he can tell us," Victor said. "Dude, he's dead. Looks like he's been dead for a long time. He didn't move a muscle."

"Hasn't got any muscles to move," Carlos said.

"I swear I've seen him move before, though," Cody said.

"Nah, Farley's probably just keeping him in there for some sort of joke," Ratface added.

"Farley doesn't joke," Cody said. "Not like this. He's Farley's prisoner. I say we should let him out."

"Yeah," Victor said. "Maybe once we let him out, he'll come rip our hearts right out of our chests at night."

"Oh, come on," Cody said. "He will not. You just said that he hasn't got any muscles to move with."

Ratface searched for a door or a switch that would raise the dome. He couldn't find anything. "Only way to get him out is to smash him out," he said. "But if we do, Farley will probably be able to guess who did it."

"What I want to know is why," Cody said. "Why is Uncle Rastus here in the dome, and what's with those other bones?"

"C'mon, let's get out of here," Victor said. "Before Farley finds us." They headed out of the lab.

"Two dead skeletons," Sully mused. "A relative and a reptile. What's the connection?"

CHAPTER ELEVEN

THE TREASURE

The boys skipped lunch the next day and headed for their old dorm room in search of their shoes. Cody and the other boys hid in the shadows around the corner and peeked out as the girls left their dorm room with magnifying glasses. Roxanne had a utility belt around her waist with all sorts of picks and instruments attached. The girls made their way slowly down the hall, still probing every door, every panel, and every brick.

"Aha!" Marybeth cried, listening to a wooden panel and rapping on it with her knuckles. "This is hollow!"

Carlos and Cody looked at each other. There really *were* secret compartments here? Cody had made that up!

Marybeth pulled a screwdriver from her belt, and in seconds had the panel removed. Roxanne shone a flashlight inside the hole.

Virginia removed a penny from the jar and examined it. "This isn't the treasure. This penny's date is only forty years old. We're looking for something older than that."

The girls put the jar back and moved off down the hall.

"Do you really think Farley stole treasure from Miss Prim?" Carlos asked.

"If he tried, he'd end up stealing his mother's dentures," Cody said. "Come on, let's go find our shoes."

They raced to their old dorm room.

"C'mon, Ratface, use your nose," Sully said. "Our shoes shouldn't be hard to sniff out. Especially Victor's."

"Watch it," Victor grumbled.

"Well, you can't deny your shoes stink like a cheese factory," Sully said. "Ratface is attracted to the smell of cheese."

"I was even before Farley turned me into a rat," Ratface said proudly.

They tore through the dorm room. No sign of the shoes. They searched under the beds and in the closets and drawers. Nothing.

They searched the bathrooms. No sign of shoes. Until . . .

"I'm not touching those," Carlos said. "Uh-uh. No way."

"Here's another toilet full," Victor said from the next stall over. "That's it. They're dead."

"*So* dead," Ratface added.

"Anyway, what about our shoes?" Sully said. "I am so sick of going barefoot. Especially with these pink toenails. Fronk and Bilgewater keep laughing at us."

"We can still trade them in for new shoes," Mugsy said. "Fish 'em out with the plunger."

"I can't believe we're actually here, picking our shoes out of the toilet, because *girls* put them there," Carlos said. "I thought boys were supposed to be the disgusting ones."

"Girls give new meaning to the word 'disgusting,'" Victor said.

"How's that plan coming for making the girls leave before the game comes around, huh, Cody?" Ratface said. "Seems to me these girls are the sticky kind. Hard to get rid of."

"Like barnacles," Victor said.

"Like tapeworms," Carlos added. "Disgusting."

"Yeah," Ratface said. "Girls are the most revolting thing there is."

"Girls make me puke," Mugsy declared.

I SWEAR I'LL NEVER TOUCH A GIRL. YUCK!
SOMEDAY HORMONES MAY MAKE US LIKE GIRLS.

BUT DEFINITELY NOT GIRLS LIKE THESE!

At field hockey practice that afternoon, Coach Howell passed out the field hockey equipment. Sort of.

"I don't think this is a regulation field hockey stick," Sully whispered to Cody. "I think it's a femur."

"A what?"

"A thigh bone," Sully explained.

Cody dropped his stick. "Yuck!"

"It's not a human bone," Sully said. He examined the stick. "Unless it was a giant . . ."

"Hey, guys, check this out!" Victor dribbled the ball over to them. "The plastic hockey ball is made to look like a skull."

Sully shook his head. "Hate to break this to you, but it's not plastic. It's a real skull."

"This isn't field hockey," Ratface declared. "It's sadistic torture! We're too young and innocent for this kind of trauma. It messes with your head!"

"Your head's already been messed with," Victor said. He swung his bony hockey stick. "I kinda like it. Nice and primitive. The way sports were meant to be."

Coach Howell blew his whistle. "All right, losers. Take turns playing goalie," he said. "Runty. You go first."

Ratface took a cautious step forward. "The goalie wears, like, full-body padding, right? And a helmet? And a mask?"

Coach Howell let out a barking laugh. "Not on my team. Only the strong survive. You ready, boys? Grab your hockey sticks. Line up. Ready, aim, fire!"

It was a brutal field hockey practice. Howell made each of the boys take a turn playing goalie, and they were completely covered in bruises by the time practice finally ended. The only reason they didn't all suffer permanent brain damage was that most of them were pretty bad at taking shots on goal.

Finally, they returned to their locker room to shower. They went to the cafeteria and ate dinner (horseradish mousse atop bean sprout and jalapeno pudding) without even noticing how vile it was.

After dinner, Cody headed for the library to look for books on flying. After a long search, he finally found what he was looking for: *Piloting Antique Biplanes for Dum-Dums*. Perfect.

On his way back, Cody took a different route, hoping to pass Miss Prim's room. Maybe, he thought, if he searched her room, he could get answers to some questions. Like why did she want to take control of Splurch Academy? What weirdo would want that?

Cody was just about to open her bedroom door when the scent of lilac perfume and a woman humming made him stop.

Weird, Cody thought.

Miss Prim popped a breath mint into her mouth from the little tin she always carried. Then she dabbed face cream onto her cheeks, pausing often to study her skin. As she did, she sang:

"Make me young and make me perky.
Magic face cream, soak right in.
Oh, my brother's foul and jerky.
Can't wait for my girls to win."

Princess wrapped her monkey tail around Priscilla's waist. "There's my sweetie pie," Priscilla said. "Aren't you, my pootikins?" She giggled. "It's good to be back in our old home, isn't it? Soon Splurch Academy will be mine once more. And when Archie-Farchie's gone for good, I'll recover all the treasures he's ever stolen from me, the greedy, little brat."

Cody backed away slowly.

So there really were stolen treasures? The girls weren't just making it up.

If what the girls said about trapdoors and passageways was true, they could be anywhere. How could he ever find out?

CHAPTER TWELVE

THE EXPERIMENT

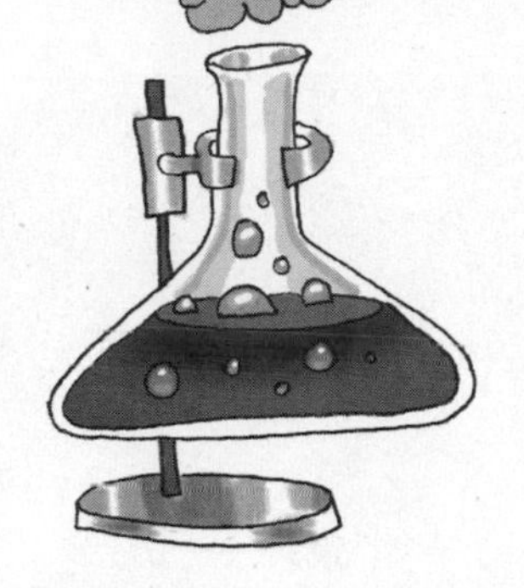

The sun had almost fully set when Cody tiptoed away from Miss Prim's door. Soon, any moment now Cody knew, the teachers would transform into their hideous monster selves and go out on the lawn to romp around, hunting and frolicking.

Down the hall, Cody saw Farley leave his laboratory. He didn't latch the door fully. Here was his chance! The door was open, and Farley was gone. He could sneak in there, smash the glass dome, rescue Uncle Rastus, and be out and long gone before Farley returned.

Cody slipped through the doorway and into the laboratory's shadows. Farley's table with the equipment and the bones was still in view. There sat Uncle Rastus, under his glass dome, looking as lifeless as ever.

Footsteps in the doorway made him freeze. It was Farley, back already. Shoot. Cody flattened himself back into the shadows. The headmaster put on a lab coat.

"Let's give it one more go, shall we?" Farley said aloud. There was no one else around. Lunatics often talked to themselves, didn't they? Farley wasn't talking to Cody, was he? Cody held his breath, praying the headmaster hadn't seen him.

"My sister thinks she's so clever," Farley muttered. He raised Rastus's dome. "Once Rover's back, she'll be singing a different tune. He's got a bone to pick with her!"

Rover? Cody shook his head. The Mongrelo-whatever. The dinosaur was named Rover.

Farley opened a closet door and pulled out a large treadmill, the kind Cody's dad used to exercise on at home. He started the motor, then plopped Rastus on the treadmill and attached cables to his skull. Then Farley attached those same cables to the small dinosaur bones and placed them on the treadmill next to Rastus. The cables ran through the strange device that looked like an old car battery with needles and wire—the Animatrometer.

Rastus had no choice but to run with the rolling treadmill underneath his feet. As soon as he ran, the dinosaur ran, too.

DIST

So, Rastus, you can *move on your own*, Cody thought. *I knew it.*

The needle on the Animatrometer hovered at MOSTLY DEAD. Farley stared at the device. "Come on," he whispered. "Come on!" But the needle never went past MOSTLY DEAD.

Farley went over to the treadmill and tried adjusting Rastus's wires. The skeleton swiped at him. The dino-dog did the same!

Whatever Rastus does, the dinosaur does, Cody thought. *It's like it's a puppet. And Farley's trying to get Rastus to bring the puppet to life!*

Farley shook his fists in the air. "You're holding out on me!" he cried. "What's your secret? I don't just want a walking set of bones! I want my Rover back!"

In response, Uncle Rastus looked away from Farley. Rover's head did the same.

Farley's shoulders sagged. He switched off the treadmill. Rastus and Rover collapsed in a heap of bones and lay there. The needle on the Animatrometer dipped to DEAD.

Farley unclipped Rastus's cables and put his dead uncle back in his dome. He ran his finger along the treadmill, where a coating of dust lay. He took a whisk broom from the wall and began tidying.

Then he stopped.

He sifted the dust through his fingers.

He looked at Rover, then at the dust.

Farley grabbed an empty glass vial from his chemistry set and filled it with the grayish powder. He mixed chemicals into a beaker, then poured the dust in.

BANG.

FIZZZZLE

Animatrometer
DEAD
NEARLY DEAD
EUREKA!

IS IT YOU?
IS IT REALLY,
TRULY YOU?
BARK!
BARK!

GOOD BOY!
WANNA PLAY
SOME BALL?

CHAPTER THIRTEEN
THE PLAN

Early the next morning in their stable dormitory, Cody told the boys what he'd seen the night before in Farley's lab. Sully, Ratface, and Carlos listened as they worked on a project—a new plan for getting even with the girls that involved snipping and bending and stitching.

"And then the little dinosaur thing came to life!" Cody explained.

"Creepy," Sully said. "But I don't see why we should be worried. A dinosaur skeleton that's the size of a dog doesn't sound any more dangerous than Pavlov."

"Yeah," Carlos said. "Rover! What a dumb name for a lizard. I'll bet Pavlov gets jealous and buries all the lizard's bones in different holes all over the yard."

They all worked busily. Carlos hammered and rigged and twisted wire, while Sully used rags, buttons, needles, and thread. Cody scribbled something on a sheet of paper.

"This is brilliant, Cody," Carlos said. "Pass me a nail?"

"The idea was half yours," Cody said generously. "Does this map look right?"

The noise woke Victor up. "What's this for?" he asked.

"A present for the girls," Sully said cryptically. "You'll see soon enough."

He handed what he'd been stitching to Carlos. "Attach those," he said. When Carlos was done, Sully stuffed everything into a bag and handed it to Ratface. "Whenever you're ready," he told him. "You know where it goes."

"Aye, aye, captain." Ratface saluted Sully and took off.

Later, at breakfast, Cody went over to the boys' old table, now occupied by the girls, and tapped Virginia on the shoulder.

"What do *you* want?" Virginia stabbed her french toast with her fork. "By the way, nice shoes."

Cody tossed a folded piece of paper onto the table. "I think we ought to have a truce," he said. "Why can't we all get along."

Virginia glared at him.

"No, I'm serious," Cody said. "I mean, you probably don't want to be here any more than we do. Right?"

SO, TO SHOW WE WANT TO BE FRIENDS, WE'RE GOING TO HELP YOU OUT.
WE DON'T NEED HELP FROM STUPID, DISGUSTING BOYS.

I KNOW YOU'RE LOOKING FOR HIDDEN STUFF. SO I THOUGHT OF A PLACE TO LOOK.
WHERE?

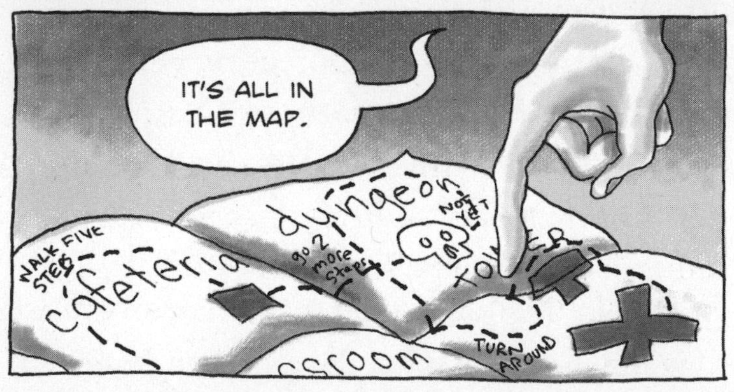
IT'S ALL IN THE MAP.
WALK FIVE STEPS
cafeteria
dungeon
NOT YET
go 2 more steps
TURN AROUND

"Good luck finding it," Cody said. "I'll warn you, it's in a dangerous place. If you're not brave enough, let us know. We'll help."

"We're braver than you are, you pinheads," Roxanne snorted.

Virginia held up a hand. "Let's give this a shot." She peered at Cody thoughtfully. "Thanks. I think."

When the bell rang for lunch, the girls exchanged secretive glances, then hurried out the door. Cody, Ratface, Carlos, and Sully started laughing.

"The fun begins," Ratface said.

The boys tiptoed after them, ducking around corners to spy on the girls.

"Down in the darkest dungeon," Virginia read from the map. "Find the trapdoor next to the water pipes."

The boys waited by the cellar door until all the girls were through the cast-iron door.

"The sewers?" Mugsy gasped. "You're sending them through the sewers?"

"Shh!" Sully hissed.

They headed down the stairs and peeked.

THAT ROTTEN FARLEY MUST HAVE HIDDEN MISS PRIM'S TREASURE IN THAT TRUNK.
WE'LL SEE . . .

BOINGG!

SPLASH!

THOSE ROTTEN BOYS!

Cody laughed so hard, there were tears in his eyes. "Brilliant!" He thumped Sully on the back. "Sheer genius!"

"Watch it," Sully said. "You nearly pushed me in."

"Here come the sewer monsters," Ratface said, pointing to the girls. "Run!"

CHAPTER FOURTEEN

THE DETENTION

"It was worth it to see those girls fall into the sewer," Carlos declared. "A night's detention chained to a brick wall is a small price to pay."

"I don't know," Mugsy said. "The stocks were growing on me. Too bad the seventh-graders were already using them tonight."

"We didn't even get to miss hockey practice for our crimes," Sully moaned. "A fifteen-mile run! My legs feel like they're made of Jell-O."

"Your legs *are* made of Jell-O," Victor said.

Cody looked around. The room they were in was on the fourth floor—one Cody had never seen before. The boys were chained to a brick wall.

It was going to be a long night.

"The game's tomorrow," Cody said. "We've got to steal that plane first thing in the morning and make our escape."

"Will you cut it out with your crazy plane idea?" Victor snapped. "You'll get us all killed. We couldn't even drive a car out of here. There's no way we'll escape in a plane!"

"Wrong," Cody said. "I've been reading my book about it. Those old planes had a lot

fewer levers and things than newer ones. No computers, even. A baby could fly one."

"*Rii-iight*," Victor said. "And you expect us to get in a plane with you because you've got a book about it. Fat chance."

"We should just let the girls win," Mugsy said. "Farley goes. They stay. We deal."

"You're nuts if you think Farley'll leave without a fight," Cody said. "If the girls win, we'll face his wrath somehow."

Victor's face went red. "Like that's anything new," he said, his voice rising. "We face Farley's wrath every day." He rattled his chains and thrashed his arms and legs against the brick wall.

BANG
BANG
I HATE, HATE, HATE, HATE THIS PLACE!

BANG
OW!

CLICK
HUH?

RUMBLE!

EARTHQUAKE!
I DON'T THINK SO...

WEIRD!

"A broom closet?" Cody said. "A secret wall just to hide brooms?"

"It's not a broom closet," Sully said. "It's like a museum. A shrine to brooms."

"Maybe that's why Splurch Academy is so filthy," Ratface said. "Someone hid all the brooms."

"At least now we know about a secret hiding place," Cody said. "That could come in handy sometime."

"What if we're stuck here forever?" Sully said, starting to panic. "What if we can't get back?"

"Hold on," Cody said. "Victor, bang your head again."

"I'm gonna have a concussion as it is," Victor grumbled. He threw back his head one more time, and the floor slowly rotated back to its original position. It stopped with a bang and a shudder.

"That was bizarre," Ratface said.

"Splurch Academy—always full of surprises," Carlos said.

A few minutes passed.

"Was I hallucinating, or did we just

find a secret hidden room full of brooms?" Sully asked.

"You weren't hallucinating, Sully," Cody said. "Not today."

"How does Farley expect us to play well tomorrow if we're chained up here all night?" Ratface wondered.

"Does it make any difference?" Sully said. "Whoever wins or loses, we'll still be here, and life will still stink."

"It'll stink way worse if we lose to *girls*," Victor added.

"We're not going to play at all," Cody said. "Tomorrow morning we're flying home in Priscilla Prim's plane."

Sully shook his head. "You're the one that's hallucinating," he said. "Dream on."

CHAPTER FIFTEEN

THE GAME

Coach Howell and Farley woke the boys up early the next morning. Howell didn't ask the boys to wake up, he just grabbed each one by the ankle and yanked him upside down.

Oh no, Cody thought. *I missed it. I missed my chance to get us all up early and fly away in Priscilla's plane. We're toast.*

"Game time," Farley said. "Rise and shine, athletes. Today you show those beastly girls what real men are made of."

Mugsy spit straw out of his mouth and sneezed. "What?"

"Meat," Coach Howell said as if in a daze. "Real men are made of red, juicy, dripping, delicious meat."

"Pull yourself together, Howell," Farley ordered. "It's breakfast time for the boys. Not you."

He pulled the lid off a cart to reveal a smorgasbord of hot, steaming breakfast food. Good stuff! It looked like Farley had ordered breakfast from a restaurant instead of having Griselda cook. It was unbelievable.

"Food!" Mugsy cried. "Lemme at it!"

Howell dropped the boys, and they attacked the food. They didn't bother with plates or forks but just shoved fistfuls of food in their mouths. But after only about five seconds . . .

"That's enough," Farley said. "Too much food and you'll play poorly. After you beat the girls, there'll be a celebration feast. If you don't . . ." Farley paused.

"You'll *be* the celebration feast." Coach Howell licked his lips.

"Quiet," Farley muttered.

Howell smeared the other boys with face paint. They put on their sneakers, took their boney hockey sticks, and followed Farley and Howell out into the cold, morning air.

The bleachers were full of the other boys from Splurch Academy as well as other girls from Priscilla Prim, who had arrived to see the game. Nurse Bilgewater, dressed in a striped referee's jersey, paced the sidelines and blew blasts on her whistle. Desdemona Chartricia Sackville-Smack, the Grand Inquisitrix of the League of Reform Schools for Fiendish Children—and Farley and Priscilla's mother—huddled in her wheelchair, bundled against the cold.

Cody felt sick to his stomach.

Ratface looked at their hockey coach, standing a ways off and licking his lips.

"Do you mean Coach Howell?" he asked.

Farley chuckled. "Worse," he told them. "Much, much worse."

He patted his jacket pocket, but all Cody saw there was the antenna of his walkie-talkie poking out.

Referee Bilgewater blew her whistle, and the boys jogged over to the midline of the field. The Priscilla Prim girls in the stands booed at them, and so did the other Splurch boys, who still hadn't forgiven the fifth-graders for bringing Farley back.

"Nice to know the fans support us," Victor grumbled.

Then the Priscilla Prim team of fifth-graders came trotting out onto the field. They took one look at Cody and his friends and busted out laughing.

"How can we play them and keep a straight face?!" Marybeth hooted.

"Hey, guys, can you loan me your makeup?" Roxanne jeered. "I left my lip gloss in my locker!"

"Eat dirt, Roxanne," Victor yelled. "You're going down."

"Ooh, Cody, was your old headmaster too poor to buy you real sticks?" Virginia sneered. "Whose bones did you use? The eighth-graders'?"

"They couldn't afford team uniforms, either," Marybeth called. "Hey, Carlos. Your tie's come undone."

"Losers, losers, Splurch boys are losers," Brittany and Brooke chanted.

Cody gritted his teeth but said nothing. He got into position.

The boys won the coin toss. The whistle blew, and Cody flicked the ball to Victor, who took off running, dribbling around Marybeth and passing it quickly back to Cody. Cody dodged Roxanne and passed the ball over to Carlos, who snagged it away from Brittany—or Brooke—and passed it back to Cody.

Hey, Cody thought. *So far, so good! We might beat the girls after all!*

Then Virginia attacked. She whizzed past Cody, snagging the ball out from under him and whacking it down the field.

Marybeth was there first. She passed it to Roxanne, who fired a goal so hard the ball punctured through the netting.

1–0, Priscilla Prim.

The stands went wild.

Farley chewed his fingernails.

Referee Bilgewater dropped the ball at the midline, and Cody passed it to Victor again—the last thing the girls would expect, he figured. Victor dribbled down the field, then doubled back and made a long pass to Carlos. Carlos outmaneuvered Brooke—or Brittany—and passed it to Cody.

Marybeth sprinted past Cody and scooped the ball up before he could get his stick on it. She fired a long pass to Virginia, who waited in perfect position.

BAM. Mugsy spun like a top as the ball whistled past him.

2–0, Priscilla Prim.

Miss Prim waved a set of pom-poms and cackled with delight while the girls slapped one another on the back.

The whistle blew. Cody flicked the ball to Carlos, who passed the ball back.

WHAM

"Foul! Foul!" screamed Farley, but Referee Bilgewater held up her hands.

"Splurch rules," she said. "All's fair."

Priscilla Prim shrieked with delight. "It was your idea, Starchy-Archie-Farchie," she cried. "Your boys are too wimpy to win!"

To everyone's surprise, Mugsy blocked Marybeth's shot on goal, and hit the ball down the field toward Ratface, the sweeper. Brittany and Brooke appeared out of nowhere, intercepting and passing the ball until they were inside the shooting circle. They set up a sweet pass for Roxanne, who fired the ball into the goal, right between Mugsy's feet.

3–0, Priscilla Prim.

The crowd in the risers went berserk, stomping and screaming. Princess did backflips in her seat.

Dr. Farley wiped sweat from his forehead.

"Okay, men," Cody yelled. "Take no prisoners! Don't hold back! We're fighting for our lives, and don't forget it!"

Virginia intercepted Carlos's next pass

and took off toward the Splurch goal. Cody chased after her. Out of the corner of his eye, he saw Farley rise to his feet and pull his walkie-talkie from his pocket.

Back in the game, Roxanne was making a beeline for the goal. Nobody could catch her. Cody's heart sank.

Then, miracle of miracles, Sully intercepted Roxanne!

It might have been an accident. Nobody seemed more surprised than Sully himself. Roxanne was almost to the goal before she even realized she'd lost possession.

"Sully!" Victor screamed. "I'm open!"

"Over here, Sully-meister," Carlos yelled. "To me! To me!"

From the corner of his eye, Cody saw Marybeth barreling down the field to clobber Sully. He had to think fast, while they still had possession.

"TIME!" he screamed. He made a *T* sign with his hands.

Bilgewater looked puzzled. "*T*-what?"

"TIME OUT, SPLURCH!"

Bilgewater blew her whistle. Cody and the other boys joined in a huddle.

"We've got to think of something," Cody said. He scrubbed his face paint off onto his sweater. "Anything! We've got to win this game! Does anybody have any tricks up their sleeves?"

Ratface reached up his sleeve. "I have some water balloons filled with Jell-O," he said.

"What on earth do you have those for?" Victor shook his head in disgust.

"You never know when things like this may come in handy," Ratface sniffed.

"I don't want to beat these girls with Jell-O. I want to beat them with muscle!" Victor pounded his fist in his palm.

"Good luck with that," Sully said. "Come on. Let's just do our cheer.

BOOM.

"Hands in the middle," Cody said. "One, two, three, gooooo team!"

BOOM.

They all stopped. The ground underfoot was vibrating.

BOOM.

The boys looked at one another.

Voices from the stands were starting to cry out in alarm.

BOOM.

ROOOAARR

CHAPTER SIXTEEN

THE DINOSAUR

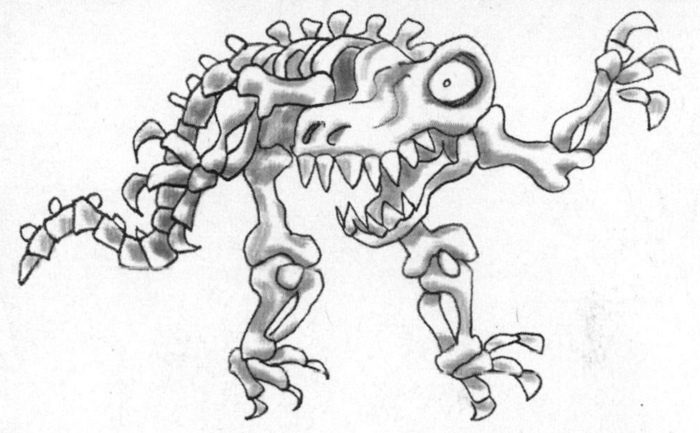

"I warned you, Cody Mack," Farley shrieked. "Sic 'em, Rover!"

The dinosaur blasted his fiery breath, and the grass became a roaring wall of flames.

Priscilla unclipped Princess's leash. The little monkey hopped and screamed.

With a jet of flaming barf-breath, Rover blasted the bleachers. They went up in flames like matchsticks.

"Run to the plane," Cody yelled. "Go!"

They heard a sound like a million bass drums.

It was Princess. *Growing.*

At the sight of Princess, the dinosaur reared back its head and roared at the sky.

In reply, the monkey bared its primate lips and shrieked a deafening battle cry.

There was a metallic scream. Cody glanced over his shoulder to see the dino-monster's massive clawed foot smash through Dr. Farley's old, repaired Cadillac like it was a loaf of sandwich bread.

Farley screamed. "Bad dog, Rover! Bad dog!"

The monster-monkey picked up the warped sedan and heaved it at the dinosaur. Its bones collapsed in a heap, then—*clackety-clack*—reassembled themselves. Rover's red eyes blazed with murderous fury. He roared at the gigantic monkey.

"Guys!" Cody cried. "Let's not stick around to watch!"

The boys ran like there was a hungry troll on their tail. They reached the plane and clambered up onto the lower wing. Cody hopped into the pilot's seat, and Victor, the first in line, hopped into the compartment behind him.

They squeezed into the plane like sardines. The playing field below looked like a war zone. Rover galloped over to the Academy and blasted it with his fire-breath. The shrubbery caught fire.

"Go, Rover!" Ratface yelled. "Go, Rover! Burn down the school!"

"Can it, doofus!" Sully yelled. "He's here to eat *us*! Don't let him hear you squawking."

Princess leaped toward the Academy building, clung to the topmost tower, and swung her body around to topple the dinosaur with a mighty kick.

But no sooner did Rover hit the ground than his bones reassembled, angrier than ever.

Cody flipped levers and flicked switches on the old plane. *How do you fly this thing?* He twisted a key. The plane coughed to life. A miracle.

"Spin the propeller!" Cody shouted.

Victor hopped out, gave a propeller blade a mighty heave, and climbed in the plane.

"Floor it, Cody," Sully yelled.

WE'VE GOT COMPANY!
WE'RE GONNA BE DINO-DOG BISCUITS!
HOLD YOUR BOXER SHORTS. I'M TRYING.

YOU SAID YOU'D FIGURED OUT HOW TO FLY!
THROTTLE? NO. GAS PEDAL? UM. JOYSTICK?

THE PLANE STARTED TO MOVE . . .
DID I MENTION THAT I GET AIRSICK?
CHOMP
CHOMP

Rover was chasing them.

"You can't outrun him, Cody!" Sully yelled. "Lift off!"

"Just a little faster . . ." Cody leaned on the throttle for all he was worth. At last, when Rover was ready to take a bite out of the plane's tail, Cody grabbed the control column and pulled back. The plane's nose rose, and she sailed into the sky.

Rover sent a fiery jet of his flaming breath after Priscilla's plane. It didn't reach the plane, but the blast of hot air made the wings flip. The plan started spinning out of control. It was like the best—or worst—amusement park ride of Cody's life.

Cody pulled as hard as he could on the control column, but the plane was gyrating wildly.

"So long, world!" he yelled. "Adios, Mom and Dad and Snarfy!"

The plane leveled just in time, and they thumped down, bouncing and skidding, right side up on the playing field.

CHAPTER SEVENTEEN

THE BODYGUARD

For a second Cody only saw colorful specks. Then his eyes focused.

The mighty dinosaur was lumbering toward them.

Then, from out of nowhere, the Priscilla Prim field hockey team appeared. They climbed up the wings and elbowed the boys aside, crawling into the overcrowded passenger bay.

"No way!" Cody yelled. He tried to block Virginia from crawling into the cockpit beside him. "This is our plane. We stole it fair and square!"

MOVE OVER, MEATHEAD. IT'S OUR PLANE AND WE KNOW HOW TO FLY IT.
BUT YOU GIRLS WILL NEVER FIT WITH THE REST OF US.

IT'S AN ENCHANTED PLANE, DUMB-DUMB.
IT CAN FIT DOZENS OF PEOPLE.

VVRROOOOOMM

Without a word, Virginia leaned into her turn and executed a neat barrel roll and loop, flying low enough to clip Rover's thick skull with her landing gear. He growled and snapped at the air.

Cody was relieved not to have to pilot the plane. "Let's get out of here," he said.

"Not without Miss Prim," Virginia said.

Cody caught sight of Farley, still talking into his walkie-talkie and grinning like the mayhem was a Sunday picnic. His mother, Madame Desdemona Chartricia Sackville-Smack, snoozed in her wheelchair, oblivious. Priscilla ran over to Farley, shouting and pointing at the plane. She walloped him with her purse.

That second, Rover stopped fighting with Princess and looked at Farley and Priscilla. He dove for the would-be headmistress of Splurch Academy and clutched her between his two clawed, reptilian hands.

"He's got Miss Prim, Virginia!" The girls seated behind Cody shrieked. "The big monster's got Miss Prim!"

Princess was out of her mind with rage. She seemed unsure of who needed protection more: Miss Prim or the girls. She chose her mistress. While Virginia circled around the Academy and swung back for another attack, the monkey dismantled Rover's tailbones and kicked a leg out from under him. But he only snapped back together again. Virginia swooped low and knocked him in the skull once more.

"That oughta give him a headache," Virginia said.

"It would if he had a brain," Cody answered.

"Have you got any better ideas?"

"Plow right into him," Cody suggested. "Chop him up with your propellers."

Virginia frowned. "What if Miss Prim gets hurt?"

Cody looked at Rover's gigantic teeth. "If you don't try, she'll get eaten for sure."

Virginia nodded, then did a loop-de-loop over the field. "Hold on tight," she yelled, gritting her teeth and clutching the control column tightly.

They swung low, flying right over the grass. "Stay on target," Virginia chanted. "Stay on target!"

Mugsy and Sully covered their eyes.

Rover looked up just in time to see them coming. He hopped to one side. The plane's wing struck Princess in the chest. The gigantic monkey bodyguard fell to the earth with a thud. The plane screeched to a halt on the turf.

"Missed!" Cody cried.

"No, we didn't," Virginia said. "We hit Princess!" She watched the fallen monster-monkey with eyes filled with tears. "She's not getting up! Princess! I can't believe I killed Princess!" Roxanne put an arm around her, too sad to speak.

The dinosaur's head shook up and down. The evil beast was actually laughing! It wagged its bony dino-tail.

Then the dinosaur held Priscilla Prim where it could get a better look at her. She kicked and screamed at it. It roared back in return, nearly blasting off Miss Prim's wig.

JUST THEN A FIGURE
CAME RUNNING
ACROSS THE LAWN.

WHAM

"Carlos, did you see that?" Cody said. "What on earth was Uncle Rastus doing?"

Virginia sniffed. "He found Miss Prim's lost treasure," she said. "She's a witch. I never knew we were searching for a stolen *broom*."

"Look at Uncle Rastus," Carlos said. "He's running back into the school. I thought he wanted to escape from there."

"Um, Cody," Sully said. "Can we fly? Rover's back for another game of fetch."

"Get your mitts off my students!" Priscilla shrieked. She sat on her broom, holding an enchanted fireball.

She flung the fireball. Rover exploded like he'd swallowed a bomb, with bones flying every which way. When the dust settled, there was a huge hole in the ground, like a meteor's crater, with Rover's bones at the bottom. "*That's* for Princess!"

But the dinosaur couldn't be beaten so easily. His bones began reassembling just as before.

Then a skeleton appeared by the side of the crater. Uncle Rastus held a lab beaker in his hand. He held it up high.

"NO!" Farley shrieked. "Not the antidote! Nooooooo!"

Uncle Rastus flung the liquid, beaker and all, onto Rover's reassembled body. The glass shattered, and the liquid fizzed and smoked. Slowly, slowly, Rover began to sway from side to side like a skyscraper in a hurricane. Back. Forth. Back. Forth.

CRASH.

Down he went in a pile of bones. And stayed there.

CHAPTER EIGHTEEN

THE TRUCE

"Thanks, Uncle," Priscilla said. She landed her broom on the grass and raced to Princess's side. The kids watched from the plane as the massive monkey shrank back down to her original size, and then lay still on the grass. Priscilla cradled her in her arms.

"Princess," Farley's sister crooned. "Princess, wake up!"

But the monkey didn't move.

Priscilla Prim reached into her pocket, pulled out her box of breath mints, and popped one between Princess's teeth.

"If you're dead, you don't have breath at all," Cody muttered. "Stinky or otherwise."

"Quiet," Virginia hissed. "Don't you know a touching scene of denial when you see one?"

But Priscilla didn't look like someone in grief. She looked at her watch like she had no worries at all. She examined her long-lost broom like it was her favorite birthday present.

"It's all over, Archie-Farchie," Priscilla told her brother. "We won the game, and the terms of the bet are set. You proposed them yourself. Don't forget to leave the keys. Pack your things and go!"

"Why, you . . . !" Farley gnashed his teeth. "The rules say the game needs two complete periods before a winner is determ—"

"Rules, schmools," Priscilla said. "Get over it. And be sure you take those hoodlum teachers of yours with you."

Just then, Princess hiccuped.

"There you are, sweetikins!" Priscilla cried. She beamed at her injured pet. "Had a nice nap? Mumsy was so proud of her heroic angel monkey!"

"You are not the winner!" Farley cried. "You robbed me of my pet. You can't have my school as well!"

He marched over to the wheelchair where their mother, Madame Desdemona Chartricia Sackville-Smack, the Grand Inquisitrix of the League of Reform Schools for Fiendish Children, and the ultimate authority behind Splurch Academy, was seated.

"Mummy!" he cried.

MUMMY, PRISCILLA SAYS SHE WON. BUT THE GAME NEVER FINISHED. TELL HER SHE CAN'T HAVE MY SCHOOL!
TELL HER ...WHAT?
SPLURCH

DON'T LISTEN, MOTHER. HE CHEATED AND TRIED TO GET HIS CREATURE TO HURT THE PUPILS.

"You said yourself that all was fair in this war," Farley retorted. "Splurch house rules. Anything goes!"

"Your team had zero points, Archie-Farchie," Priscilla said. "My girls were annihilating your boys before you brought out your little pet to gobble up all the athletes." She stroked Princess's fur. "Besides, your monster died and mine didn't. So that makes my school for total winners." She smirked. "Your school's for total losers."

Farley scowled at his sister. He tugged on his mother's sleeve. "Say something, Mummy!" he pleaded. "Tell Priscilla to take her nasty girls and go home!" He stroked her arm. "I'll make you your favorite hot toddy with extra molasses."

Priscilla Prim made a noise of disgust. "You're pathetic." She stroked her mother's other arm. "Mumsy, dear, I'll make you crab apple scones drenched in butter."

Desdemona Sackville-Smack's droopy eyes rolled back in her head. "Time for my nap now," she said.

Her head drooped. Madame Sackville-Smack drifted back to sleep.

"You see? You see?" Priscilla was triumphant. "She said, 'Listen to your big sister.' That means I win!"

Their mother's eyes opened once more. "Hmph? Huh? What? What'd I say?"

Priscilla hopped up and down. "You said Archie should listen to me. Which is like saying I'm in charge. And I won the game, anyway, so I ought to be in charge. And . . ."

"Share," Desdemona said. She smacked her lips together and sighed. "Someone, wheel me to my room. I'm so tired. Share, you two. Or you'll wish you had."

"I *won't* share with her," Farley declared. "I won't, I won't, I won't . . ."

Priscilla wailed like a little girl. "Mother, I can't share with Archie! You know I can't! He's a lying, sneaking, underhanded little beast! And a bad dresser. Mother, please, *please* don't make me do it. Mother!" She shook her mother's shoulder until the ancient woman woke up once more.

"Can't a body get any rest around here?" Desdemona snapped. She raised a menacing finger. "NOT another word. Or I'll send you BOTH to time-out for teasing your poor old mother! Now, wheel me in."

The adults marched off toward the building, leaving the kids to climb down out of the airplane by themselves.

"I want that hot toddy and the buttered crab apple scones you promised," Madame Desdemona told her children. "Don't think for a minute that I wasn't listening."

Cody and his friends stood around, not sure what to do. The Prim girls did the same.

UM, GOOD GAME.

HUNH.
YOU GUYS STINK.

AT FIELD HOCKEY, I MEAN.
GEE, THANKS.

They headed toward the school along with all the other kids. Cody'd already looked around to see if they could escape by foot, but the regular Splurch faculty were prowling the perimeter of the property for just that very reason.

"Come to our room later on today and we'll give you a bottle of nail polish remover," Virginia said. She studied her own fingernails as if she were bored.

"Okay." Cody kicked at a pile of fallen leaves. "Good thing you don't have to search for that lost treasure anymore."

"Look," Virginia said. "Let's get one thing straight. We still hate you guys, okay? All of you. Hate your guts right through and through to the rotten core."

Cody scowled. "Yeah, well, we hate you first and hate you worse!"

"Don't think just because we've had"—Virginia made quotation marks with her fingers in the air—"*a moment* with you turkeys, that now we're friends. Because we're not."

"I never said we were!" Cody said.

"Every chance we get, we're gonna whup your sorry hides," Virginia said. "In sports. In spelling bees. In science fairs. In every kind of competition you can think of. And a bunch I'll bet you can't think of, you big bunch of pea brains."

Cody folded his arm across his chest. "Who're you calling *pea* brains, you Priscilla Prim girls? P. P. girls? Hey, get it, guys? Pee-pee girls!"

"That's right," Ratface squeaked. He started an obnoxious chant. *"Sew-er! Sew-er! Sew-er!"*

"Okay, pee-pee girls," Cody said. "You think you're such hot stuff? Game on."

A cold wind blew in from the west that afternoon, covering the sky in thick, brooding clouds. The boys could hear Farley throwing a tantrum in his laboratory, smashing beakers all afternoon, while Ivanov hobbled around the playing field, picking up debris one piece at a time.

Ratface and Carlos came into the stables laughing.

"All the girls' showers will be freezing cold now," Ratface giggled.

"And sudsy," Carlos said. "We cut off the heat for their hot water heater and poured a whole bottle of dish soap into the tank."

"High-five, man," Victor said, holding up his hand for Carlos.

Cody's heart wasn't in the fun. "What difference does it make, guys?" he said. "Our escape plane needs major repair. We couldn't get rid of the girls. We couldn't even get rid of Farley. That would have been a pretty cool consolation prize. We've been humiliated in sports, and now we're stuck sleeping in manure-filled stables forever."

"Look on the bright side, Cody," Sully said. "Rover's dead again. Getting chewed up by an angry dino-dog would have been a lousy way to die."

"Yeah," Mugsy said. "And if we're stuck having girls around, at least Farley's stuck having Priscilla around. She drives him bonkers. That'll be kind of fun to watch."

Sully tugged on Cody's sleeve. "Look outside," he said.

Cody looked out the window and saw Uncle Rastus arm in arm with a skeleton wearing a faded hat and a feather boa. They disappeared into the trees.

"Aunt Rhoda!" Cody said. "Whaddya know."

"At least someone's happier now," Sully observed.

Cody thought about it. He had helped Uncle Rastus, hadn't he? Freed him from Farley's clutches? That was worth something. He hoped it was, anyway.

"Let's go to dinner," Cody said. "I heard the girls requested lasagna to celebrate their victory."

"Griselda's burnt lasagna," Ratface said. "My favorite."

"With ketchup," Mugsy said.

"And tomorrow morning, let's just happen to be passing by our old dorm," Carlos said with a mischievous grin, "right about shower time."

R.I.P.
AGAIN,
ROVER

Acknowledgments

Special thanks to our niece Sophia Smith for the hard work and the cheerful company, and for knowing how to decorate a girls' dorm room. Thanks also to our nieces Elspeth and Claire Newton for painting their father's toenails pink while he napped.

About the Authors

Sally Faye Gardner and Julie Gardner Berry are sisters, both originally from upstate New York. Sally, who now lives in New York City with a smallish black dog named Dottie, has, at various times, worked as a gas pumper, janitor, sign painter, meeting attendee, and e-mail sender. Julie, who now lives near Boston with her husband, four smallish sons, and tiger cat named Coco, has worked as a restaurant busboy, volleyball referee, cleaning lady, and seller of tight leather pants. Today she, too, attends meetings and sends e-mail. Julie is the author of *The Amaranth Enchantment* and *Secondhand Charm*, while this is Sally's first series.